Margaret Rome

BRIDE OF THE RIF

MILLS & BOON LIMITED
LONDON · TORONTO

First published 1972
Australian copyright 1979
Philippine copyright 1979
This edition 1979

This edition © Margaret Rome 1979

ISBN O 263 72921 4

Set in 11 on 13 pt Linotype Plantin

Made and Printed in Great Britain by
C. Nicholls & Company Ltd,
The Philips Park Press, Manchester

CHAPTER I

THE bows of the luxury cruise ship *African Queen* were cleaving the waters of the warm Mediterranean en route for Tangier. Her upper decks were ablaze with lights, laughter, music and happy voices spiralled noisily aloft, then were hushed – swallowed into the surrounding darkness of the tropical night. It was playtime for the passengers aboard, the time of day when children slept and relieved parents were allowed to snatch a few hours of pleasure not attuned to the demands of their offspring; time for the middle-aged to sink gratefully in the depths of the nearest comfortable chairs and to relive in retrospect the wonders revealed on earlier sightseeing excursions; and for teenagers, the much looked-forward-to hour when the day's exploratory skirmishes with the opposite sex, the tentative smiles and interested glances, reached fruition in the seclusion of the upper boat deck.

By comparison, the atmosphere inside an upper deck lounge contrasted sharply. There, the only sound that impinged upon the concentrated hush enveloping the room was the thrumming of the air-conditioning and now then a smothered cough – quickly suppressed when the culprit was made aware of accusing eyes swivelling momentarily towards him, then back again to the card game taking place inside a circle made up of eager, enthralled spectators. Sara Battle did not so much as blink when her companion called his opponent's bluff.

"I'll see you," he challenged casually in the vernacular familiar to card-playing addicts. No evidence of prize money was apparent, no chips littered the table nor was there any currency in sight, but the watchers gasped as they acknowledged the cool professionalism, the casual indifference to the winning or losing of an invisible stake which they were aware amounted to a small fortune, displayed by the handsome, elderly gentleman and his aloofly beautiful young companion.

The young Spaniard who had been challenged bit his lip and hesitated momentarily, then, with a defiant flourish, he spread his cards face uppermost on the table. "Three aces and two queens!" he offered a trifle wildly. "You've beaten me every night this week, Colonel, but this time I think it is my turn to scoop the pool!"

Dismayed shock caused Sara's wrist to jerk and connect with the stem of a wine glass set near to hand. Luckily, she managed to grab it in time to prevent its contents from spilling over the table, and the sigh of relief that rippled over the waiting crowd owed its origin more to a release from tension than to any dismay felt at the thought of damage caused by spilt wine. But almost immediately attention was again riveted upon the two players. Sara made a valiant effort for control and her features resumed their usual mask of composure, but she could not suppress the quiver of relief that relaxed her mouth when the Colonel, with his customary aplomb, spread out a Royal Flush and countered mildly, "I think not, Don Alvaro, tomorrow night, perhaps . . .?"

Colonel Battle took the following storm of congratulations in his stride, but even within the circle of admiring well-wishers Sara was conscious of a wave of disapproval emanating from a man standing aloofly apart who made no attempt to add his congratulations to those of the excited throng. As she glanced up their eyes collided, and his look of frowning distaste sent a shiver through her tense body. Each night for the better part of a week he had appeared in the lounge just as the games were about to start, and his forbidding presence had acted as a spur on her already tender conscience so that her usually nimble fingers had become numb as she shuffled and dealt the cards and her quick wits had become so dulled the Colonel had twice sharply reprimanded her for making some stupid move. Only that evening, before they left the dining-room to start playing, he had reproved her,

"I hope I can rely upon you to pay attention tonight, Sara, because if I can't I would prefer that you drop out of the game altogether rather than saddle me with a partner whose moves would shame a beginner at a village whist drive. What ails you, girl, are you sickening for something?" She had known she could not hope to fight his deliberate obtuseness. Many times she had tried, and failed, to get him to see her point of view, but there was no way of penetrating his stubborn refusal to see reason. Perhaps that was why her argument had lacked spirit when she had replied.

"Yes, I am sick! Sick of travelling around the world, sick of having no permanent home – no chance to put down roots – and most of all I'm sick of playing cards, especially when I know it's our only means of existence and that we have to *win to live*!" The Colonel's moustache had bristled and for a moment Sara had shared the same feeling of trepidation that had been felt by many young subalterns unfortunate enough to have incurred the Colonel's wrath while under his command. He had then drawn himself stiffly erect and, in a manner reminiscent of the way in which he had enforced discipline during his many years' service in India, had snapped,

"You're being impertinent, dammit, and I will not tolerate impertinence!" He had glared at her across the table, making no attempt to hide his fury so quickly, and before his peppery temper could escalate into a second eruption, she had risen to her feet and with as much dignity as she could muster had begun walking towards the exit. Luckily, very few passengers had opted for the second sitting for dinner and the dining-room was fairly empty, but even so a rush of shamed colour had stained her cheeks as she had weaved her way between the tables, pretending to ignore the many curious glances.

Once inside her cabin she had paced the floor, furiously angry, wondering, not for the first time, why she tolerated such an alien existence. For five years, since the age of fifteen, she had accompanied her grandfather on his everlasting cruises. At first it had felt as if a dream had come true. For as long as she could remember an orphanage had been her home. When she was a mere infant her father and mother, both only children, had been killed together in a car crash. The authorities had tried without success to find some relative who might claim the child who had been thrown, still in her carrycot, unharmed out of the crushed car. But when no one had come forward she had been taken to the local orphanage where for fifteen years she had grown up thinking herself completely alone in the world. Then had come the wonderful day when she had been summoned to the matron's office where a visitor had been waiting to meet her. She had felt instinctively drawn towards the elderly gentleman who was introduced as her grandfather because even though at first sight he had looked stern – even forbidding – his hands when he had taken hold of hers had been shaking with suppressed feeling and as he had bent down to kiss her proffered cheek his eyes had filled with unashamed tears of emotion.

Explanations had followed much later, after the dust of the orphanage had dropped for the last time from her feet and she had been escorted by her grandfather into the cabin she was to occupy for the duration of her very first cruise. She had been too excited to take in his words, too grateful to him for transporting her into a Cinderella world to wonder at his earlier lack of concern for his family, and so she had accepted without question the circumstances he had outlined as an excuse for his neglect. To her, it sounded quite feasible that on being discharged from the Army he should have chosen to remain in India to try to find some occupation which would enable him to stay in the country he had come to love. But India had had nothing to offer the man who had spent the better part of his life in her service, and then had begun his years of drifting. The fact that he had ceased to receive letters from his only son had caused him some misgivings, he had told her, but being a poor correspondent himself, he had shrugged off niggling doubts and nursed an inward conviction that his son was probably too busy with his own affairs to bother about a father he had not seen for years. It had been mere chance, when the ship on which he had been travelling had made an unscheduled stop at an English port, that caused him to come ashore on a lightning visit only to discover that Sara, the last of the Battles, had for years been languishing in the care of kind, but unavoidably austere, officialdom . . .

She had been inside the cabin only a few minutes when a tap on the door had heralded the crisp command: "Sara, open up, I wish to speak to you!" With a shrug, her temper no longer at flash point, she had moved obediently towards the door.

"Come in, Gramps," purposely she had used the affectionate term that never failed to please him, then found herself having to suppress a smile when his scowling countenance had softened into a sheepish smile. With a lightning change of mood so characteristic of the Battles he had reached out to hug her before ruefully apologizing. "I'm sorry about that disgusting display of temper, child, forgive me. . . . ?"

She had answered his request with a smiling nod, but even so his brow had creased into worry furrows and his arms had dropped from her shoulders. Testily, he had begun to grope in his pocket for the case that held his cheroots and without his customary request for permission he had lighted one, then blown a savage stream of smoke from pursed lips before making the surprising admission,

"You're perfectly right, you know, Sara, I should be horsewhipped for introducing you into the sort of life we've led all these years." She had tried to contradict, but he had silenced her with a gesture. "No, somehow, without realizing myself quite how it happened, I slipped into the routine of a professional gambler. It was the only thing I was good at, you see." After a dejected shrug he had qualified hastily, "Other than military practices, that is. I pride myself I did my job well in the Army, but," the glowing tip of his cheroot had been examined minutely while he sought for words to

11

justify his weakness, "the Army doesn't equip one for the ardours of civilian life. Unknowingly, soldiers become cosseted from such things as money worries, where to live, where to work . . . To a regular soldier the Army is a home, family, employer, and when you are cast out – no longer needed," he grimaced bitterly, "it's similar to a non-swimmer being thrown in at the deep end. One clutches at any straw for survival."

Quickly, Sara had moved to his side, her face contrite. "Stop it, Gramps, do you hear? I won't have you blaming yourself. You've been wonderful to me and I'll always love you for it, always!" Her last words had ended in a choked sob and she had leant her head upon his chest to hide from him the tears she was fiercely ashamed of.

"Don't try to whitewash my actions!" he had clamped, determined, once having admitted his guilt, to purge his soul completely. "I've used you abominably and you know it! From the age of sixteen the only art you've been taught is that of playing cards. I've passed on to you every bit of skill I possess and you've learnt your lessons well – I'd defy any man in the world to better you when you are playing on form. But you're right to feel ashamed, because it's not exactly the sort of skill one looks for in a young and beautiful girl. You have a right to expect better things and in future, dammit, I'll see to it that changes are made. You've partnered me for the last time, Sara. From now on I play alone!"

12

Her head had jerked up at these words. His face had looked flushed, too highly flushed, and she had felt a twinge of fear. He was so upright and so handsome still, with brilliant, far-seeing eyes and thick iron-grey hair, that she was apt to forget he was far from young. If anything should happen to him she would be once more on her own. The thought was unbearable. Anxiety had made her voice sharp as she had demanded,

"Sit down and stop talking foolishly, Gramps. You know you couldn't bear to live anywhere else but afloat, and card-playing is the only way we have of stretching your pension far enough to pay my fare. I've a right to earn my keep, so of course I must help out! Besides that," she had faltered ... "I like to play."

His blue eyes had looked straight through her, deep into her innermost soul. "Little liar," he had grunted. "You're a disgrace to your namesake and you know it!" She had smiled wanly at this reference to an oft-repeated private joke. Many times he had quoted to her a passage from one of Lamb's "Essays of Elia" in which a character named Sarah Battle considered that "Whist was her life's business; her duty; the thing she came into the world to do, and she did it. She unbent her mind afterwards over a book". But while Sara often took refuge in a book she did so in an effort to rid herself of the guilty remorse she felt each time she relieved some amateurish card-player of his money.

When a vagrant sigh had escaped her the Colonel's

13

frown had deepened and a determined line had appeared between his bushy eyebrows. "I meant what I said, Sara," he had growled roughly, "in future I play alone. And I promise you," his direct look had been as binding as a pledge, "that as soon as we have sufficient funds we'll leave this life behind us and settle down somewhere ashore. Will that please you, d'you think, my love?"

Half laughing, half crying, she had run to hug him.

"Oh, Gramps!" For a moment she was quite incapable of forcing the words of delighted agreement passed the lump in her throat, but when she did finally manage to speak he was left in no doubt of her joy and heartfelt relief. "You'll never regret your decision, Gramps, I promise you," she had babbled happily. "We'll find a house somewhere – near the sea, or perhaps in the country where you can go for long walks and fish or shoot game – and I'll cook and clean and look after you so well you'll wonder why we wasted all these years! Oh!" a visible shudder had run through her tense young body, "just think how wonderful it will be when there's no more need to pretend we're rich, bored tourists who advocate playing for stake money merely to add more spice to the game! If you only knew how much I've hated the subterfuge we've had to practise in order to avoid being exposed as gamblers . . . the deceit, the lies, the occasions when we've even had to sink so low as to *bribe* members of the crew not to give us away to the captain . . ."

14

She had faltered to a stop when she had felt him go rigid. Her outburst had shaken him to the very depths, her vehement words had stripped bare his way of life and for the first time he was forced into facing reality – to see himself portrayed not as the cultured sophisticate he imagined himself but as a petty adventurer, a cheap gamester who, if his intentions were known, would never again be allowed aboard any ship belonging to a reputable shipping line. Appalled by her own insensitivity, she had tried to stutter an apology. "Gramps, I've hurt you! ... I didn't mean ..." But her words had not seemed to penetrate; with granite-hard features, his lips compressed into lines of shock, he had turned from her and marched, with his back ramrod straight, out of the cabin ...

The clamour of excited voices escalated into a discordant babble and Sara suddenly felt that if she did not get away she would scream. Her grandfather was still enclosed within a circle of congratulatory onlookers, and her silent antagonist had disappeared, so she slipped out of the lounge and sped towards the bow of the ship, searching the deeply-shadowed deck as she ran for a corner that might offer the solitude she craved. When at last she found a deserted spot she leant against the rail and waited until her thumping heartbeats had subsided and her riotous thoughts could be marshalled into some semblance of order.

She was worried, dreadfully worried. The Colonel had stuck to his resolution not to allow her to play that

15

evening, so she had had no other option but to sit, re-
belliously, watching the game. Gradually, a sense of
foreboding had begun to plague her. No reason, other
than some sixth sense, was responsible for the depres-
sion that descended like a dark cloud, causing her to
cast many worried glances in her grandfather's direction. But he seemed to have recovered his former spirits
– indeed, he radiated such an aura of well-being her
fears were calmed – until she noticed his feverish flush
and the light of reckless abandon that had replaced the
grave intentness he usually displayed when a game was
in progress. A faint suspicion that he might have been
drinking was dismissed instantly; he never drank before a game. Not even the relief she had felt when the
young Spaniard, Don Alvaro de Leon, a reckless young
man who always insisted upon playing for enormous
stakes – had been beaten was enough to dispel the sense
of impending doom that gripped her so mercilessly she
found herself trembling as she stood gripping the ship's
rail with hands grown suddenly cold.

When an icy voice snaked out of the darkness she
spun on her heel with a frightened gasp.

"You look like a sea wraith standing there, *señorita*.
I was almost afraid to speak in case you should vanish
over the side at the sound of my voice. Why are you so
edgy, I wonder? Could it be that you are plagued with
remorse?"

Her startled eyes fastened upon the shadow that was
moving towards her out of the darkness and when it

was near enough to take substance she backed away and choked out a confused: *"You!"*

"Yes, it is I, *señorita*," he bowed distantly. "Don Felipe de Panza, cousin of the young fool Don Alvaro de Leon whom you helped to rob this evening!" As she stared mesmerized at the tall, haughty Spaniard whose silent disapproval had plagued her for a week Sara wondered wildly if she was experiencing a nightmare from which she would shortly waken. But there was nothing ethereal about the man who now stood mere inches away, searching her face with anger-dark eyes that contained in their depths a smouldering flicker of danger.

"Well, do you deny my accusation?" the hateful voice continued, "or are you searching for excuses – an exercise at which I am sure you are adept."

"Please," her constricted throat refused to allow more than a whisper, "I don't understand. Are you accusing me of cheating?"

"As an accomplice you are every bit as guilty as your," he paused, then drawled with distaste, "companion. It was he who did the actual switching of cards, but please do not ask me to believe that your unfortunate accident with the wine glass was not intended as a deliberate diversion created solely to enable him to change his hand during the few seconds that all eyes were upon you!"

When this outrageous meaning finally penetrated she erupted into a flare of white-hot anger. The dark mane of hair seemed fairly to bristle and her eyes, twin orbs of sparkling emerald, lighted furiously upon his darkly-etched features in the manner of trained artillery with sights set to blast him from the face of the earth.

"*How dare you!*" Even as she spoke her hand connected with his lean cheek in a slap hard enough to rock him on his heels. Surprise was the element responsible for the success of her attack, and for the amazement that held him silent while a dull red mark spread across his cheek.

"You she-devil!" He reached out and caught her shoulders in a bruising grip. Tight-lipped with fury, he bit out: "If you were a man I would kill you for that!"

"And if I were a man," she twisted abortively in his grasp, "I'd never rest until I'd made you eat the disgusting lies you've just spoken!"

"Lies, are they?" Her heart almost stopped beating when he jerked her head erect and forced her to face the full battery of his rage. "Then if they are lies, why is your accomplice being escorted at this very minute to the captain's cabin to answer the charge of cheating which I personally have laid against him?"

"*No!*" Her eyes distended with horror as his words reverberated like a crash of doom in her ears. Through narrowed eyes he watched the signs of shocked incredulity and unbelieving dismay that drained every drop of colour from her face. When his grasp slackened she twisted from his hands and retreated to stand pressed, like an animal at bay, against the ship's rail. For a

18

second she fought gallantly to suppress tears, then, after a shuddering sigh, she flung at him accusingly, "If what you say is true, if you really have done such a despicable thing – *I shall hate you for the rest of my life!*"

CHAPTER II

SARA ran all the way to the captain's quarters, hoping dementedly that what Felipe de Panza had said would prove to be a lie, that the threat he had uttered in his anger had been born of a vicious desire to frighten her. But when she reached the captain's cabin and flung open the door, forgetting in her anxiety to knock, the words she heard confirmed what she had inwardly suspected – not even in anger would the arrogant Spaniard be prepared to lie.

The captain's stern voice was directing her grandfather: "Not only did you blatantly disregard company rules by inveigling fellow passengers into playing for stake money, but worse, much worse, you set out deliberately to cheat and rob those who were unfortunate enough to be conned into playing your game!" His eyes flickered momentarily across to Sara, acknowledging her presence without giving her a chance to intervene. "If it were not for your granddaughter here," he nodded in her direction, "I would be tempted to put you ashore at the next port of call and leave you to your own devices, but because of her – and *only* because of her – I'll be lenient. You can both remain aboard until the cruise is ended, but you will not at any time be allowed to mix with the rest of the passengers. The crew will be instructed to see that my orders are carried out, so I would advise you not to disobey my command, because if you do I shall have no alternative but to carry out my original intention which was to order you off this ship!"

At these words, Sara's temper boiled over. Taking a hurried step forward, she blazed up at him, "How dare you accuse my grandfather of cheating! He may have broken your rules, but cheat? Never!"

The captain returned her furious look with unrelenting firmness. "I'm sorry, Miss Battle, but your grandfather was seen by the passenger who reported him to switch cards. It seems this same gentleman has been keeping a very close watch on Colonel Battle because he was somewhat sceptical of his unusually long run of luck. He suspected him of being a cardsharper, and to-night his suspicions were confirmed. Naturally, he reported what he had seen to me, and when your grandfather submitted to a search by one of my officers a playing card was found lodged in the lining of his coat sleeve."

Sara fought waves of shock to protest. "But finding a solitary card upon his person doesn't prove anything. It's only Señor Panza's word against my grandfather's . . ."

The captain was not used to having his decisions questioned. Frostily, he replied, "Don Felipe is a well-known and greatly respected member of a very old Spanish-Moroccan family. I have the honour of having been personally acquainted with him for many years and can vouch that he is a just, honest man of great integrity; not a man who would bring serious charges against another without being very sure of his facts, but one I would trust without doubt or question. So, Miss Battle, as I have no intention of discussing the matter further, I will be obliged if you and your grandfather will go to your cabins so that I can continue with my work."

It was a peremptory dismissal; the captain was not the most tolerant of men and the contempt that showed in the manner in which he turned his back and began rifling through the papers on his desk would have been found galling by all but the most insensitive. To the Colonel, who up until then had seemed rendered speechless, the captain's attitude was intolerable and he gave vent to his resentment in a burst of blustering defiance. With a roar reminiscent of the barrack square, he attacked the startled captain.

"You, sir, can keep your favours for those spineless enough to accept them! You have the audacity to set yourself up as judge and jury – I've been tried, found guilty, and sentenced – all upon the word of one Felipe de Panza who you yourself admit is a personal friend of yours! Well, I don't intend that the matter shall end here. Tomorrow, I shall write to the chairman of the Line and complain forcibly about the treatment I've received on this ship! And as for your ridiculous decree that we must spend the rest of this cruise segregated from the rest of the passengers – I refuse absolutely to accept it! What have you to say to that, sir! "

Sara closed her eyes and prayed the captain would be lenient. Although she agreed with every word her grandfather had said, she could not help but wish he had chosen a more diplomatic way in which to put his objections before a man who, if anything, seemed even more arbitrary than he was himself. She felt a sick feeling in the pit of her stomach when the captain's haughty face flushed a dull red, and was hardly surprised at his icy reply.

"I say this, Colonel! Tomorrow we dock at Tangier. Please see to it that all your belongings are packed ready to be transported ashore first thing tomorrow morning. You've worn out your welcome aboard this ship! "

The next morning she felt a fierce gladness when she realized they were to be spared the humiliation of being banished in the sight of curious eyes. The ship was anchored off Tangier when an early breakfast was served to her in her cabin by a blank-faced steward who informed her that a tender would be waiting to take herself and the Colonel ashore in an hour. Between them, they had quite a lot of baggage. The life they led necessitated smart, up-to-date clothes to help perpetuate a wealthy image, but as she had packed everything possible the previous night, when the time came for them to disembark they were able to board the tender without fuss and without any but a handful of passengers taking a pre-breakfast stroll around deck being any the wiser.

She sat stiff-backed, fighting a wave of humiliated tears, as the tender sped away from the ship and the coastline of rocky cliffs and sandy beaches grew gradually nearer. But by the time she was being helped on to the quayside at Tangier she was sufficiently composed to pretend an interest when the Colonel pointed out to her an old Arab town perched on top of the hill sweeping down towards the harbour. When he hailed a taxi and began directing the driver to one of Tangier's most expensive hotels, she began an involuntary protest, but then she bit her lip and managed to remain silent while she inwardly resolved that before the day was over she would confront him not only with a demand for an explanation of the catastrophic events leading up to their banishment from the ship, but also for a detailed and truthful account of the state of their finances.

The room she was given was quietly luxurious. Cool white walls, white lace bedspread, and a white lattice-work canopied bed were saved from monastic severity by a vividly patterned tiled floor. Tall windows with protective white shutters opened on to a view of bright blue sea, bobbing yachts, and a sweep of green hillside crammed with white-painted villas each surounded by an expanse of garden profuse with blossoms of riotous colour. As she stood absorbing the view a vagrant breeze whisked dusky tendrils of hair across her furrowed brow, then advanced to tease with a dry-sounding rustle the leaves of a large potted palm stood effectively against the stark walls. The rustling sound interrupted her train of thought, and with a decisive gesture she turned on her heel and made towards the door. Unpacking would have to wait. Too many questions were seething around in her mind – questions which, for the sake of sanity, her grandfather must be made to answer immediately!

His room was just along the corridor from her own and in a matter of seconds she was outside his door demanding to be let in. When, after a few hesitant seconds, he appeared, she saw by his expression he was braced for argument, so without preliminary she began her attack.

"I have some questions that must be answered, Grandfather," she told him firmly as she settled down in a chair and showed every indication of refusing to budge until she received satisfaction. He looked affronted, he was usually the one who gave the orders and she the one who obeyed them, but the sparkle in her green eyes warned him to be cautious, and suddenly, after a moment of rebellious silence, his stern mouth relaxed into a smile and he sat down facing her. His manner, when he began searching his pockets for his cheroot case, appeared nonchalant, but to her dismay she saw that his hands were trembling.

"You're right, my dear, the hour of evil is upon me,

explanations can be put off no longer. But I warn you – you will not like that you're about to hear."

A chill sidled down Sara's spine even as she confidently assured him, "You have no need to deny the accusations made against you, Grandfather – you're quite incapable of cheating, I know that. What I want you to tell me is how the misunderstanding occurred in the first place, and what steps you intend taking to clear your name. Señor Panza must not be allowed to get away with his despicable actions, he must be made to publicly apologize for daring to sully your good name with such a foul fabrication of lies!" She stopped, her breast heaving, her face flushed with angry indignation, and glared across at him as if he were the instigator of her fury rather than the insolent Spaniard whose name she had spat out as if the mere mention of it burnt her tongue.

Under her furious gaze he seemed visibly to wilt. Stilts could have been kicked out from under him as he sagged against the back of his chair. Misty film clouded his eyes and lines appeared around his mouth which she had never suspected were there. His usually stabbing look was a mere flickering of his eyelids as he glanced up and then quickly away before nerving himself to take some tremendous strain.

"Señor Panza didn't lie, Sara," he told her heavily. "I did wrong, God help me, but I did it with the best of motives. Unfortunately, I was found out."

Incredulously, she stammered, "Grandfather! This

is no time for jokes, please don't tease ..." Her words ended in a choked gasp when she saw his face whiten and his knuckles stand out as he gripped the arm of his chair.

Compulsion to justify his actions, to banish the shocked horror from her eyes, brought words tumbling from his lips. "I did it for us, Sara, so that we might realize a dream. Alvaro de Leon is a compulsive gambler – a wealthy playboy with money to burn. The amount staked on the game we played was a trivial amount to him, but to us it represented a cottage in the country, a chance to settle down and live a normal life with normal people! " When her fixed gaze did not alter he sighed and began to plead. "Try not to blame me too much, Sara. Despicable though my action might seem, it was not premeditated, I swear it! Alvaro had a good hand – I sensed that – but I was only an ace away from having an unbeatable one, a royal flush, and your accident with the wine glass seemed a God-sent opportunity which I seized upon almost without thinking. In the space of a split second, the thought became deed and for the first time in my life I cheated an opponent. Do you believe that, Sara?" he urged with a momentary return of his customary dignity. "Do you believe me when I say it was the one and only time in my life I've ever cheated?"

His bowed head and agonized eyes were too much for her. With a passionate cry she dropped to her knees beside him and cradled his drooping body in her strong young arms. "Of course I believe you, Gramps!" she rasped through a throat tight with compassion. "It was all my fault for trying to change your way of life simply to satisfy my own selfish whims! You took me from the orphanage and introduced me to a life of luxury such as I'd never dared dream about. Travel, good food, beautiful clothes, you gave me all of these as well as an abundance of love, and I repaid you with dissatisfaction and continuous nagging to change your ways. Don't dare to reproach yourself ever again, Gramps. The blame is mine – all mine!"

He murmured soft denials while he stroked her bent head and waited until her storm of remorseful tears was spent, then when she was calm enough to think clearly he supplied the answers to the other question she had intended to ask.

"About money, Sara . . ."

"Yes, Gramps?" She went very still.

He cleared his throat and began, "We have very little capital left – enough to pay our hotel bill for little more than a week, in fact." When she drew in a gulping breath to speak, he hurried on, "I know what you're going to say, and I don't agree. You would have us move into some cheap sleazy hotel without decent food and no air-conditioning, but to my mind that would merely be prolonging the agony. I much prefer to live in a decent hotel for a week rather than exist in an inferior one for a month."

"But what will happen when the money is finished?"

she asked in a voice registering panic at the hint of returning obstinacy she saw in his outthrust chin.

"I have a plan," he returned confidently. "It's a huge gamble, I admit, but desperate situations call for desperate measures. The Club Aziz in Tangiers has always been an exceptionally lucky place for me. I intend going there tonight, taking what cash we can spare, and I guarantee, my love, I'll bring back enough money to get us back to England and, if my luck runs true to form, some to spare!"

She stared at him with wide, frightened eyes, wondering if she had heard aright. To be stranded in a place like Tangier with hardly any money was bad enough, but to deliberately contemplate risking what little they had on a card game was criminally foolish! Only then did she realize how deep the gambling bug had bitten into her grandfather's soul. In a voice she found difficult to control, she charged him,

"You'll do no such thing, do you hear me?" When his chin lifted a degree higher, she stood up and held out a trembling hand. "I want every penny we possess in my keeping and I want it now, Grandfather. For both our sakes, I must insist that you hand it over immediately!"

For an agonizing moment she thought he was going to refuse, but then, with an offended shrug, he pulled his wallet from his pocket and threw it down in disgust upon the table. "Take it!" he flung across his shoulder as he strode furiously from the room. "I never thought

I'd see the day when a Battle would succumb to cowardice! I hate to quote clichés, but as you well know 'Live for today' is a motto I've always found pleasing. Think on it, Sara. You have plenty of time before the club opens in which to change your mind!' "

For the rest of the day his parting words reverberated in her mind, but her resolution never faltered. If she had been under his influence during her most formative years perhaps his devil-may-care attitude, his reckless disregard of the need for caution, would have rubbed off on her, but orphanages rarely breed frivolity, nor even over-confidence, and Sara's inherently cautious nature revolted against encouraging him in his rash venture. To occupy her mind – and to avoid running the risk of being subjected once more to the influence of his persuasive tongue – she decided to explore Tangier. Shore excursions had not been included in the itinerary of their life aboard the luxury cruise ships because they were expensive extras and, in any case, as the Colonel had stated bluntly: "Pickings are better aboard."

She thrilled to many new sights and sounds as she wandered unaccompanied through the steep, narrow streets of the old town. Everywhere she looked, old contrasted with new, women in European clothes mingled with veiled Arab women; pale-skinned merchants in expensive suits rubbed shoulders with dark, fierce-eyed men in *djellabahs*, who wore their robes with aristocratic arrogance; donkeys with full panniers sauntered along in the path of monster cars whose abundant chromework drew the sun like a magnet so that eyes had to be averted from stabbing rays reflected from gleaming coachwork. She was enthralled by her first sight of a water-carrier in his elaborate, crazy gear. On his head he wore a wide brown and red straw hat hung all around with charms and baubles. As he walked, small bells and glass ornaments jingled at every step, and added to that was the clashing of brass cups which he wore on a long string around his neck. When he swung towards her she took his piercing cry as an effort to attract her custom, but although she was thirsty she dared not chance drinking the water he carried in a goatskin slung over his shoulder. Firmly, she shook her head and was relieved to see him turn without demur and stroll away looking like a cross between a clown and a walking fountain, ringing his handbell vigorously as he went.

After wandering for hours, oblivious to time, it was a relief to find a garden with seats placed at strategic spots for the benefit of the public. A burning feeling at the back of her heel had begun throbbing in earnest, so she tottered over to the nearest vacant seat and eased her sandal strap away from what she imagined must be the beginnings of a blister. The garden was high on a hill overlooking a wonderful view of shipping far below in the Straits. In the distance she could make out the outline of the Rock of Gibraltar, and opposite, a mere ten minutes away by plane, was the brown,

parched coast of Spain. She frowned, her pleasure
spoilt by a transient reminder of something unplea-
sant. Reluctantly, she began recalling to mind the lean
facial contours, the firm mouth and despising e͏ es of
Felipe de Panza. A lump lodged in her throat as she
remembered the utter contempt in his voice when he
had accused her. Ignorant of the truth, she had stood up
well to his searing indictment, had retaliated nobly in
defence of her own and her grandfather's honour, but she
flinched when she remembered the pistol-sharp sound
of her open palm connecting with his lean cheek. The
proud señor would never forgive that humiliating slap . . .

Shivering, even under the caress of the hot African
sun, she began limping out of the gardens to make her
way back to the hotel. The scarlet of hibiscus, the
purple and crimson of bougainvillea, the silvery euca-
lyptus trees and the green leaves and golden fruit of
the orange trees all merged into a kaleidoscope of colour when a sudden rush of tears blurred her vision. In
the midst of her dejection a thought brought a measure
of relief: for one thing, at least, she could thank the
captain – his edict that they should leave the ship had
spared her the ordeal of a second meeting with Señor
Panza – the idea of having to endure his scathing condemnation while knowing it to be *deserved* would have
been more than her proud spirit could have borne.

The Colonel was very morose that evening at dinner;
he evinced no interest whatsoever in the account Sara

gave him of her afternoon's activities, but answered merely in monosyllables without bothering to look up from the food he was moodily pushing around his plate, Finally she lost patience with him.

"Are you going to sulk all evening, Grandfather? Because if you are I might as well go straight up to my room."

He shrugged, unrepentant. "And I might as well do the same. I wouldn't care to sit in the bar knowing I dared not allow myself to become involved with people. I've been hard up many times in my life, but never so much that I couldn't afford to buy an acquaintance a drink!"

Sara felt remorse. By depriving him of his money she had hurt his pride as well as his pocket and his aggrieved attitude was his way of showing it. "Very well, Gramps," she sighed, "you shall have your money back if you'll give me your solemn promise not to be extravagant. You do realize," she leant forward to give emphasis to her plea, "that this money is all that stands between us and starvation?"

His eyes lit up as she handed over the wallet she was carrying in her handbag for safe keeping. "Of course, I realize that fact only too well, child! You've no need to worry, I intend to make this money stretch as far as possible."

She left him contentedly sipping an after-dinner brandy and went upstairs, meaning to spend the evening with a book. But the written words danced meaninglessly before her eyes, refusing to make sense while chaotic thoughts chased through her mind. Finally, after deciding that physical effort was needed to counteract the tension building up inside her, she tossed it aside and went into the bathroom to wash her hair. Shampooing, setting and drying out helped to dispose of the better part of the evening and by the time her glossy black hair was combed to perfection footsteps outside the hotel, together with jovial goodnights exchanged between friends, denoted the return of fellow guests from their evening activities.

She sighed, conscious of her own loneliness. She had made very few friends aboard ship and certainly no lasting friendships. Not from any lack of opportunity, because the atmosphere aboard ship is the friendliest in the world; nowhere does one mix more freely or advance more quickly into deep relationships. It was for that very reason she had had to don a mask of reserve, to gain an undeserved reputation for aloofness; it was the only way to save herself the embarrassment of having to evade confidences, or even telling lies, in order to avoid making public the fact that she and her grandfather had no permanent home, no solid, respectable background. Impatiently, she threw down the comb and swung sharply away from the sight of her mournful eyes and drooping mouth reflected in the mirror; she needed company to help restore her spirits and in that respect, at least, her grandfather never failed her.

There was no sound coming from inside his room

when she knocked tentatively upon his door. She knocked again, sharply this time, and when still she received no answer her heart began to pound with heavy, frightened thuds. For no particular reason her grandfather's last words popped into her mind. *I intend to make this money stretch as far as possible*, and only at that moment did she recognize a possible *double entendre*, to begin to suspect that they might have been chosen deliberately to hide his true intention which, by his own admission, was to risk every penny they owned on a game of chance!

With frantic haste she picked up the telephone, but when the desk clerk asked politely if he could be of assistance she found it impossible to keep her voice steady when she asked him to page Colonel Battle.

"Colonel Battle? He left the hotel about two hours ago. I telephoned myself for a taxi to take him to the Club Aziz."

The blood slowly drained from her face as she digested his words. The shock was so great that for a second she could not move or speak, and it was only when the desk clerk's anxious voice had asked for the third time whether she was all right that she found the courage to whisper, "Please will you get me a taxi? I must go after him."

"But, Miss Battle," he sounded perturbed, "the Club Aziz is not one I would recommend that you visit without an escort. What if your grandfather should have left . . . ?"

35

Her brittle laugh startled him as much as the hardness of her answer. "He'll be there – get me that taxi immediately!"

Even the taxi driver seemed reluctant to leave her when he finally drew up in front of a badly illuminated house surrounded by depths of shadow in which a dozen different dangers might have lurked. The street was narrow, dark and crooked, the roofs of the houses just saved from touching by a narrow slit of sky only one shade lighter than the inky depths of the old town beneath. But she refused to be dissuaded from entering the club, nor, as she had just enough money to pay his fare, would she allow him to wait, so when she ran up the steps and disappeared through the entrance he shrugged his shoulders at the folly of the English and drove away.

She hardly noticed the extreme garishness of her surroundings as she moved quickly towards a flight of stairs leading upwards. From sounds she could hear as she ascended, she judged it was not the sort of place her grandfather would visit from choice: his taste leant towards quieter, more dignified surroundings, and the high-pitched female voices that were rising above tortured strains of music coming from an inferior band somewhere above were ample indication that whatever luck he had been favoured with on previous visits to the Club must have been great enough to overcome his distaste for the prevailing unsavoury background. She had reached the top of the stairs and was about to enter the main room of the club when a black-sleeved arm was thrust in front of her.

"I'm sorry, *mademoiselle*," a pleasantly accented voice informed her, "but you cannot be permitted entry without showing proof of membership." The young Frenchman who barred her way looked as if he would be more at home in wide open spaces, his vibrant eyes echoed the blue of summer seas and his tanned, handsome features evidenced that he was no stranger to sun and spray.

"Please," she stammered, appealing to the hint of sympathy she saw in his eyes, "I must find my grandfather. I was told he came here."

The young man's smile faded when he heard the tremble in her voice and his expression became grave. "Then we must do what we can to assist you, *mademoiselle*. But first, let me introduce myself. I am Marc Rochefort, temporary assistant manager of this club. I will be happy to enquire around the premises for your grandfather if you will tell me his name?"

"Oh, thank you so much, *monsieur*, if only you would! My grandfather's name is Colonel Benjamin Battle."

"Then our search is ended before it is begun." Sara saw relief in his smile. "There is a card game taking place in one of our private rooms and only minutes ago I heard one of the gentlemen inside being addressed by that very name. Come —" He held out a guiding hand. "Let me show you the way."

She followed him along a corridor and when he stopped outside a door and indicated that they had arrived her body stiffened with apprehension. She was shaking when she stepped inside the room, hardly daring to search for her grandfather amongst the men who sat around a circular table, totally engrossed, for fear of what she should see written on his face. When she eventually did nerve herself to single him out her heart plummeted. There was no need to count the pitiful stack of chips that lay in front of him; his expression was enough to warn her that the thing she had tried to prevent had already happened. Even as her eyes swept over him, noting his grey pallor, the nervous twitching of his lips, he looked up and saw her.

"Sara!" He half rose from his seat as he croaked out her name then, for long, terrible moments his mouth worked as he fought for speech. Before her horrified eyes he seemed to crumple, then, with one last penitent look, he toppled forward to lie spreadeagled across the table. The next moment the room was in an uproar. Sara knew she screamed, because the sound of it echoed in her ears for hours afterwards, but her limbs refused to obey the instinct to move and she could do nothing but stand with shock-widened eyes watching her grandfather being lifted from the table and lowered gently on to a settee. As Marc Rochefort swiftly loosened the constricting tie from about the Colonel's neck, he rapped out an order to one of the men to fetch a doctor, then almost in the same breath commanded another to fetch brandy. When this was brought, he put an arm behind the Colonel's shoulders to lever him forward and manage to force a few drops of the spirit through his blue lips.

When Sara saw his eyes flicker, the blood began to flow once more through her veins and with a sob of relief she ran forward and dropped to her knees beside him.

"Gramps," she quavered. "Oh, Gramps darling, are you all right? How do you feel?"

He responded to her frightened appeal by moving his hand a fraction towards her so that she could clasp it in her own. His lips moved, but his breath was coming in laboured gasps and the effort to speak seemed quite beyond him. Marc pressed her shoulder, warning her not to encourage him to talk, so for ten long minutes until the doctor arrived she sat quietly, his hand in hers, devouring his pain-whitened face with eyes full of dawning fear.

Marc took her to an adjoining room when the doctor arrived and insisted that she should sip a glassful of brandy while she waited for the results of his examination. She was hardly conscious of her surroundings, much less of the man who had taken her so competently into his charge, but she obediently swallowed a minute quantity of the spirit although without once moving her eyes from the door behind which her grandfather was lying.

As soon as the doctor reappeared, she jumped up and

ran towards him. "How is he? Please, tell me quickly.
. . ."

Again, Marc Rochefort's steadying hand was there
to support her when the doctor answered gravely, "He
has suffered a severe heart attack. I have given him an
injection which will help alleviate the pain, but he is
very weak. However, he insists upon seeing you, Miss
Battle, and to avoid over-exciting him I had to agree.
An ambulance should arrive within the next few minutes, so until then you may sit with him."

With a quickly gasped: "Thank you, doctor," she
ran past him into the room. Blinds had been drawn across the windows and one small lamp cast a dim pool
of light on to the colonel's drawn, but now peaceful
face. He opened his eyes when she tip-toed across to
the bed and for a fractional second his glance went
beyond her to where Marc Rochefort stood. His puzzled
eyes assessed him, then slowly lightened with relief,
but his attention was all for Sara when he enunciated
slowly, "I'm sorry for the mess I've made of things,
child. Please forgive me?" She shook her head in vio-
lent repudiation of his need to apologize and buried
her tear-stained face against his arm. But he persisted,
and she was forced to listen. "You are so like your
mother, Sara, so lovely . . . But she never approved of
me, you know. She would have much preferred, if she
had known, that you should spend the rest of your life
in that orphanage rather than come under my influence,
and who could blame her? I've been selfish," he laboured

on even when she gestured him to be quiet, "so selfish and so criminally stupid I don't deserve to be forgiven ..." When his voice petered out she lifted her head with a startled jerk, but he made a tremendous effort and continued, "We've always had to fight for survival, you and I," a faint mockery of his usual grin lifted the corners of his mouth. "Battle by name and battle by nature, eh?" he quipped with a pitiful attempt at humour. "But at least you have an indomitable spirit and the fiery nature you inherited from me will help you combat the hostilities of life; I comfort myself with the thought that whatever rigours lay ahead you will meet them with unbowed head and an unbroken spirit." She shivered at the finality of his words. Her lips parted to assure him of her love and complete dependence upon him, but before she could speak the doctor strode into the room followed by two attendants who transferred the Colonel to a stretcher, then took him downstairs to a waiting ambulance.

She was allowed to go with him in the ambulance, and Marc insisted upon accompanying her. All during the long night while she sat tense and silent in the hospital waiting room, jumping at every footstep and flinching at every unexpected sound, he talked continuously as though in an effort to release her from her nightmare thoughts.

She was grateful for his understanding, for his lack of curiosity towards herself and her grandfather, and most of all for his company during her long vigil, and

41

she turned instinctively to Marc to hold her hand while she nerved herself to meet the approaching doctor.

The doctor looked haggard when he entered the room, his white coat creased and his hair flopping untidily across his furrowed brow. His eyes were so full of pity that she knew he was searching for words to soften a blow, so she put him out of his misery. White to the lips, and feeling unbearably cold, she whispered, "He's dead, isn't he . . . ?"

"Yes," he sighed. "We did everything we could; he lost consciousness almost as soon as we arrived here and although we fought all night to preserve a last flicker of life, it was no use . . ."

She mustered all her courage and choked, "He believed in living one day at a time. I'm glad he managed to live this one to the full." Then she turned towards Marc and was enfolded into his waiting arms.

CHAPTER III

OF necessity, interment is swift in the tropics and twenty-four hours later Sara was trying to cope with the bewildering knowledge that she was now totally alone in the world. The situation would have been daunting enough in her own country where at least she would have known where to begin to pick up the threads of her shattered life, but here in Tangier – a cosmopolitan city teeming with foreigners, birds of passage too engrossed in their own affairs to give a second thought to a stranded, bereft girl whose only assets were a trunkful of expensive clothes and an aptitude for playing cards – it was frightening in the extreme. If it had not been for Marc Rochefort she might have floundered in a welter of despair; even when he suggested a possible solution she was too numbed with shock to properly appreciate his plan.

They were lunching together at her hotel when he broached the subject of her future. Watching as she prodded a fork through untouched food on her plate, he frowned and chided gently, "Please try to eat something, Sara, you've had nothing for two whole days. Won't you make an effort – to please me?"

Her eyes were vague when they lifted to his face.

"What . . . what did you say?" She shook her head and made an effort to concentrate. "I'm sorry, Marc, I wasn't listening, I'm afraid. I wonder you bother to seek me out when I'm such depressing company."

"I am worried about you, Sara," he said. "Forgive me if I intrude, but I must ask. Have you sufficient money for your needs?"

She swallowed hard. "I have the money from the chips you cashed belonging to Gramps." She faltered at the memory of that fateful last game, then hurried on, "There's enough to pay my hotel bill, but there are funeral expenses to be met and my fare home . . . perhaps if I sell some of my clothes . . . I shall have to find a job, but first of all I must move from this hotel and try to find somewhere less expensive. Perhaps you know of a cheap *pension* in the French quarter, Marc? All I shall need is one room."

He frowned. "I could ask the *propriétaire* of my *pension*, but you would find it a great change from what you have been used to." He glanced quickly around their luxurious surroundings, comparing them with the clean but strictly functional amenities of his own lodgings, and wondered how the contrast would strike her.

She read his mind. "I am sure your *pension* will be no more spartan than the orphanage where I spent the first fifteen years of my life. I haven't always been used to luxury such as this."

His eyebrows rose in surprise. She fitted so perfectly

the·part of an indulged child of fortune that it was
hard to imagine her in any other setting but one of
wealth. Her clothes were expertly styled and obviously
expensive, her shoes and handbags looked as if they had
cost as much as he earned in a month, and it was hardly
possible to believe that her skilfully manicured hands
with their perfectly shaped nails could ever have carried out menial tasks. Her disclosure helped to stifle the
doubts he felt about the suggestion he intended to put
to her. So he cleared his throat and offered: "There is
a vacancy at the club for a croupier, if you are interested?"

Her first instinctive reaction was one of dismay The
club's brash atmosphere and coarse clientele had re-
pelled her at first sight and the thought of becoming
part of it was abhorrent. When he saw her hesitation,
he pressed on, "I know the Club Aziz isn't your scene,
Sara, but I would be constantly at your side to protect
you from any unpleasantness, although, to be fair, I
doubt if there would be any. Our patrons are not out of
the top drawer, I admit, and some of them do tend to
over-indulge themselves with liquor, but on the whole
they are well behaved and I'm certain that when you
get to know them you'll find them as likeable as I do
myself. Certainly, I would not like the idea of your
working there alone, but you'll be quite safe under my
eye and the money offered is too good to be overlooked
– far more than you'll get anywhere else in Tangier."

A refusal stopped on her lips at this reminder. She

had no skill to offer any employer; gambling was all she knew, and much as she longed to cut free from the association she was sickeningly aware that she had no choice but to carry on, for a while at least, if she were to survive. Silently, he watched signs of inward conflict chase across her expressive face. "Very well, Marc, I'll do it."

"Good!" He reached across the table to give her hand a reassuring squeeze. "I'm selfishly glad to hear you say so because it means I shall see more of you than I would have done if you had decided to opt for a job during the day. I'll hire a boat, we'll swim together, and sunbathe, and I'll show you parts of Morocco the ordinary tourist doesn't know exists. You won't regret your decision, Sara, I promise you. We are going to have a marvellous time!"

He proved to be a man of his word. During the weeks that followed he gave all his spare time to banishing painful memories from her mind. He introduced her to his many friends amongst the predominantly French-speaking hoteliers of the town. She moved from her hotel into the house of Madame Blais, Marc's landlady, a small, neatly-proportioned Frenchwoman whose heart was bigger than her frame, and when sun-filled days were followed by nights of feverish activity as she threw herself into learning the intricacies of her new job, her agony gradually faded and she began once more to be able to face the world with a modicum of self-confidence.

Her extensive wardrobe was a decided asset to her job. Each night she dressed carefully before going to the club, taking as much care with her hair and her make-up as she would have done if she were about to attend some important function. Her perfectionism paid off in a surprising way. The management noted that die-hard drinkers whose behaviour had given them much trouble in the past seemed very anxious to gain favour with the new croupier and rather than risk seeing her delightful nose turned upwards at the sight of them, they were curtailing their intake of alcohol to within reasonable limits. This change caused no loss of revenue, because the table Sara managed was crowded with eager gamblers almost from the first night she took over and in no time at all word of her charm and skill circulated and became a magnet that drew clients from all over Tangier into the Club Aziz.

Marc was delighted with her success and told her so one night as they drove to the club. He took his eyes off the road long enough to admire the rich emerald sheen of her dress as it contrasted eye-catchingly against burnished hair piled high over her forehead and swept into a sophisticated pleat at the back of her head.

"I'm not surprised the club is being inundated with requests for membership," he teased. "Your appearance has not only bemused the clients, it has brought out in them a latent desire to appear as gentlemen – in your eyes at least." He chuckled and drew deeply on his cigarette. "There has even been a suggestion from one of our directors that we rename the club – he thought The Cleopatra might be apt. Are you flattered?"

The grin was wiped from his face when she replied in a tight voice, "No, I'm not flattered to be linked to a queen who brought ruin in her wake! No one knows better than I how near to disaster is a man with gambling in his blood. Isn't it bad enough that I'm forced to earn my living encouraging men to gamble without having to endure jokes about a situation which is already tormenting my conscience?"

He muttered a soft imprecation and drew the car into the side of the road. Catching hold of her shoulders, he forced her round to face him, his usually merry eyes dark with dismay. "You sound as if you hate your job, Sara? I had no idea . . . I thought you had enjoyed these past few weeks . . ."

She drew in a deep breath and admitted shakily, "I do hate it, Marc, not the club, nor the people I meet there, but having to encourage men to become victims of the gambling syndrome. It's a disease, Marc, a horrible, gripping disease that grabs a man's soul and takes him over completely! You may find it hard to understand because you've never been bitten by the bug, but for the past few years I've lived in the centre of an international brotherhood that ordinary card-players know nothing about. It's not just money that entices hardened gamblers to the tables – the excitement of bluffing an opponent gets into a man's blood! Many times I've watched my grandfather going through the ritual of looking into a man's face and smiling even though the cards in his hand amounted to practically nothing – and smiling the same way when he was certain he was going to win. It's a cat and mouse situation where the biggest bluffer takes all. The trouble is, once a man becomes hooked he's hooked for life and then, as my grandfather used to say, is when Old Nick takes over." With bitterness, she jerked out, "And I'm the go-between – the one who makes it all possible!"

"No, Sara!" He shook her. "You have magnified the situation out of all proportion. The club is not the den of iniquity you imply, it is merely a place of relaxation, somewhere to while away a few pleasant hours!" But when she shook her head, unconvinced, he had to recognize the guilt and remorse that plagued her. "Very well," he conceded, "if you feel so strongly that what you are doing is wrong, and I cannot convince you otherwise, you must stop working at the club." She began a protest, but he held up his hand for silence. "You need not worry about finding another job. I have friends who will help you if," he became thoughtful, "it should become necessary."

"You know I can't leave," she appealed despairingly "I still need the money for my fare to England and I wouldn't earn half as much doing any other job."

"Must you return to England? Couldn't you, instead, come with me to France as my wife?"

"Marc! I never once thought . . . I like you tremendously, but . . ."

He pulled her forward into a quick comforting embrace. "I understand, please don't distress yourself, Sara. I've loved you since the first night we met and I've hoped ever since that you might come to love me, but I see now I was foolishly optimistic. I hesitated to tell you earlier," he confessed, "because I think I knew inwardly what your answer would be. However, my father has sent word that he wishes me to return home to take over the running of the business. It seems he has not been well lately, and his doctors have advised him to rest. Naturally, I shall have to go, but I put off making a final decision so that I might have more time with you." He flicked away a tear that clung to the edge of her long, thick lashes and forced himself to look away from her infinitely kissable mouth that was trembling with the hurt she was feeling for his sake. "Although I must accept that you cannot return my love, Sara, I have one favour to ask of you which, for the sake of my peace of mind, I hope you will not refuse. Will you allow me to pay your fare back to England? If you cannot bring yourself to accept, then I must cable my father not to expect my return just yet because I refuse absolutely to leave you alone in Tangier."

She met his intent look and realized he was deadly serious. For one wild moment she was tempted to accept his unexpected offer of marriage. He was everything a girl could wish for, handsome, attentive, kind, and so thoughtful of her feelings that she despised herself for not being able to spare his. She could not return his love because her own feelings were dead, she told herself fretfully; she was nothing but a shell, a vacuum, empty of all emotion.

Marc deserved only the best, and the little she had to offer was an insult to his generous nature. But it was inconceivable that he should ignore the wishes of his father simply because her pride baulked at the idea of taking his money. For his sake, she had to overcome her scruples.

"Thank you, Marc," she replied with dignity. "I can accept your offer of money because, contrary to what you believe, I do love you. There's no one in the world closer to my heart. You're a wonderful, very dear friend and I should hate to have to stay here in Tangier without you."

"Sara." Gently he lifted up her chin and touched her lips with his own. It was a sweet kiss, haunting as a goodbye, and it brought a rush of tears to her eyes. But he would not allow them to fall. Deliberately, he dispersed the atmosphere of almost unbearable emotion by ordering firmly, "No tears, *ma petite*, we have customers to think about, remember? They come to see you looking radiant, so for the short time you will be remaining at the club we must try not to disappoint them, eh?" His tanned, handsome face was blurred by tears, but she managed to satisfy his demands by nodding agreement before he started up the car and drove off in the direction of the club.

It was even more hectic than usual that night, and

Sara was kept so busy she had no time to dwell upon the unhappy fact that she was shortly to be deprived of Marc's bolstering presence. She had quickly learned the routine of the club, and had progressed from presiding over chemin de fer, baccarat, and roulette until, by popular demand, she now worked almost exclusively at the table set aside for the confirmed addicts – the poker-players. It was midnight when the game that was in progress broke up and she was able to slip away to take a half hour's break before play re-commenced, to continue until the early hours of the morning. She was making her way to Marc's office where she knew a tray of coffee and sandwiches would be waiting, when a familiar voice called her name. Blood pounded in her ears as she slowly turned to face the man who had hailed her.

"Sara! Sara Battle! What a pleasant surprise, I had no idea you were in Tangier!"

"Señor de Leon! I, too, am surprised. I thought you were still aboard the *African Queen*. What brings you here?"

The young Spaniard dismissed the question she so badly wanted answered and flashed her a wide smile.

"Alvaro, please. We were not so formal aboard ship and Señor de Leon sounds as if you no longer consider me a friend! I had nothing to do with the unfortunate misunderstanding that was the cause of yourself and the Colonel having to leave the ship, I hope you believe that? Where is the Colonel, by the way? I would very much like to match skills with him again." They were surrounded by noise, hemmed in with people, and being jostled on all sides so that coherent conversation was impossible, so after a slight hesitation she suggested:

"Would you care to join me for coffee? We can go into the office and talk without interruption."

A few minutes later, settled in a comfortable chair and supplied with coffee, he repeated his former question. "Is the Colonel here? I would very much like to meet him again."

"No, he isn't," she answered abruptly, knowing herself incapable of discussing her grandfather's death without showing distress. The pain of it was still too new, the wound too tender to stand even slight probing, so she deliberately allowed him to misunderstand.

"Oh, I'm sorry to hear that," Alvaro frowned his disappointment. "I have never played against a cleverer opponent and I was so looking forward to a return bout. I shall never forget our last game," he missed her sudden flinch. "It was, without a doubt, the most exciting I have ever played and, although I lost, I feel I excelled myself that evening simply because the Colonel's skill brought out the best in me."

"You didn't lose," she whispered. "My grandfather cheated, you know that."

He shrugged. "What of it? I might have done the same in the circumstances. I've no doubt he needed the money desperately or it would never have happened. Certainly, I would never accept my cousin's ridiculous

53

assertion that the Colonel was a professional cheat — he was too much of a gentleman. No, he was tempted and he fell, but I have too many weaknesses of my own ever to judge him. Only a person such as my cousin Felipe, who has never been known to digress from his rigid standards, has a right to condemn us lesser mortals," he bit out savagely.

She strove to sound casual, but her hands were tightly clasped when she asked, "And where's your cousin now? Is he with you in Tangier or did he continue the cruise alone?"

"Felipe on a cruise?" he laughed without humour. "I assure you, *señorita,* my cousin would not waste his precious hours on such a frivolous project. His presence aboard ship was deliberate. He was following his usual practice of tracking me down simply to exert his authority as head of the family and order me to return home where, as he so grimly put it, he intends to see that I shoulder my share of responsibilities. Our family is one of the richest in Morocco, yet he thinks he can compel me to work in the vineyards like a common labourer. I must learn the business from the bottom up, he says, otherwise my allowance will be cut to nothing!" He glowered into his empty coffee cup, but after a few moments' silence his frown vanished and he chuckled. "But I have fooled him. He thinks I am asleep, worn out with honest toil, and look at me," he waved his hand to encompass his surroundings. "How his temper would erupt if he could see me now!"

Sara heard him out, feeling growing dismay. It took great effort of will to question him further. "Where is your home, Alvaro? Is it near Tangier?"

He nodded. "Actually, we have several. My mother and Felipe's, who are both widowed, live together at our family estate just across the Straits in Spain itself. We also have extensive vineyards to the east of Tangier, on the slopes of the Rif mountains – a benighted spot where nothing ever happens – and that is where my dear cousin thinks I am at this very moment incarcerated while he himself is preparing to entertain at his villa on the outskirts of Tangier a young woman whom he has decided I will marry. What a hope!" he exclaimed furiously. "Do you wonder I am tempted to choose the most unsuitable bride I can find as a lesson to him that we are now living in the twentieth century? I must find some way to impress upon him that I refuse to recognize his right to decide when, where, and even whom I am to marry!"

Sara was appalled. She had been left in no doubt that his cousin Felipe was an arrogant, forceful man, but that he should think himself qualified to choose the woman his cousin should marry was too imperious even for him. Alvaro's resentment found an echo in her own heart. Reckless and ineffectual he might be, but he deserved better than to have to live his life under the thumb of a despot, a man whose tremendous conceit made him intolerant of the weaknesses of others.

Alvaro was gratified by the sudden warmth she gen-

erated as she offered him more coffee and hastened to
light a cigarette he raised to his lips. He was used to
such attentions from the opposite sex, but up until now
Sara's manner had held a hint of aloofness, a cool contemplation that had at times left him feeling uncomfortable and slightly inadequate. He preened himself,
certain her change of heart was a tribute to hidden
qualities she had only just recognized, completely unaware that she saw him as a victim of oppression, a
martyr who needed help to escape the clutches of the
man she blamed for the untimely death of her grandfather.

CHAPTER IV

Two days later Marc left for Paris. He booked on the first available flight after receiving a telegram which told him his father's condition had deteriorated and that he was asking to see him. Sara accompanied him to the airport and waited with him in the lounge until his flight was announced.

"Are you sure you don't mind being left alone, Sara?" he asked for the umpteenth time, glancing again at the hands of his watch that were creeping inexorably towards the time of separation.

"Of course not," she said with a smile. "Madame Blais will look after me and I promise you I'll book a passage for home as soon as they find replacements for us at the club. You know we agreed we couldn't both leave at a moment's notice, it would put the management in too much of a spot, so I'll stay on for another few weeks, at least, to give them time to engage new staff. So please, Marc, do stop worrying. I'll be perfectly all right, I assure you."

He jumped to his feet when an announcer's voice boomed across the lounge informing him and his fellow passengers that it was time to assemble at the departure gate. Grasping her shoulders, he questioned with renewed urgency, "The cheque – your passage money – is it safe? Do you have it with you?"

"Oh, Marc!" Knowing he would not leave until he had assured himself that she still had the cheque he had given her the previous evening, she scrabbled in her bag and withdrew it with so much haste that it escaped her light-fingered touch and fluttered to the floor, coming to rest at the feet of one of the approaching crowd. Both she and Marc made a dart towards the precious piece of paper, but the man whose shoe it touched was quicker. Even before it had time to settle, he picked it up and began scanning its contents with eyes so intent Sara knew they were missing neither her name nor the amount payable to her from the account of one Marc Rochefort. She pulled up short, her heart somersaulting, then like the clashing of swords her eyes met those of the man who was holding the cheque between thumb and forefinger as if its proximity was offending.

"Yours, I think, Miss Battle," he offered icily, his patrician features mirroring distaste.

She wanted to scream a denial of the conclusion he had so obviously formed. Each time they met it seemed she was surrounded by incriminating circumstances and now, if looks could be taken as evidence, she was once more being judged a ruthless gold-digger out to prey upon the susceptibilities of men. She had never hated him more than when she had to swallow his unspoken insults and accept meekly the cheque he was holding out towards her.

"Thank you, Señor de Panza." She snatched the damning piece of paper from his hand and thrust it into her bag before slipping her hand through Marc's arm and edging him in the direction of the departure gate. "Please excuse us, we must go or my friend will miss his plane."

Felipe de Panza bowed, his quick glance taking in every detail of Marc's distrait appearance, then he turned to walk back to his waiting companion.

She missed Marc dreadfully, but never more so than the first evening when she worked alone in the club. Without her having realized it he had become a buffer; his protective manner had served to warn off anyone who would have attempted a more familiar approach towards the attractive new croupier, with the result that, once his absence was noted, she began to sense disturbing undercurrents in remarks addressed to her by some of the club's more unsavoury characters.

She was dealing cards, preparatory to beginning a round of poker with three of the club's most valued clients – Tangier businessmen who discarded respectability as quickly as unwanted cloaks once they crossed the threshold where their names were synonymous with reckless gambling. One of the men, hard-eyed, softly-spoken and indefinably distasteful, had tried often to ingratiate himself in the past, without success, but this evening his manner was so much more familiar, his lascivious eyes so revealing, that Sara knew he was aware of, and was rejoicing in, the absence of her protector. She suppressed a shudder when his hand reached out to enclose hers in a clasp that was moist and clammy.

"May I have the pleasure of your company at supper tonight, my dear?" he hissed through teeth so large and tobacco-stained she was reminded of weathered tombstones.

Her face felt stiff as she tried to smile. "You are very kind, but I already have a supper engagement."

"So?" The angry flicker in his eyes told her he knew she lied. "May I ask with whom?" His clasp tightened when she tried to withdraw her hand, and when her quick desperate glance of appeal towards his two companions was met with broad grins her heart sank. She had no wish to make a scene; instinct told her that in a showdown with the management her own value would balance lightly against the weight of currency poured into the club by her three tormentors, and although Marc's generosity had helped enormously, she was still in need of money to pay one or two outstanding debts, so she dared not risk being dismissed.

"A . . . friend," she faltered, attempting once more to tug her hand free of its trap.

"But your friend Marc Rochefort left today," he persisted with enjoyment, "and everyone knows you have no other close friend in Tangier."

"Then everyone is wrong, *amigo*!" The voice came from behind her, and she spun round quickly to meet the laughing eyes of Alvaro de Leon. Then, as his glance slewed round to her companion, his smile faded and in a voice incredibly like his cousin's he observed, "The *señorita* does not seem to find your company amusing, gentlemen, so perhaps it would be as well if you were to seek your pleasures elsewhere." The following undignified scramble to vacate seats underlined forcibly the power wielded in Tangier by Alvaro's family; a family of money and position, the possession of which seemed to give even to its weakest member the strength of Atlas, in the sight of these men, at least.

She was shaking so much she was barely coherent when she thanked him. "I'm so grateful for your help, Alvaro. That man – he was so horrible, I couldn't cope..."

"Then why do you try?" A frown sat uneasily upon his usually cheerful face. "I simply do not understand, *señorita*, what you are doing in this place. It is not for you, ladies do not frequent such places as the Club Aziz! Why, in my country, if a girl were to be seen even entering such an establishment she would be forever damned in the eyes of the family of any prospective suitor. Never would she be allowed to live down the disgrace!"

Her sense of humour revived at the sight of his shocked face; for all his earlier bravado, his tirade against the resistance of his cousin to modern trends, Alvaro himself was still a century behind in his attitude towards women.

"Then perhaps it's just as well I have no suitor at

61

my heels," she teased. "Just imagine how it would shock your cousin, for instance, if you were to tell him you were paying court to a girl who earns her living as a croupier in the most notorious club in Tangier! The mind boggles at picturing his reaction."

To her surprise he did not join in her laughter, but sat staring at her across the table, his eyes fastened upon her face with startled intensity.

"Is something wrong, Alvaro? Why are you staring at me like that?"

He jerked back to reality, but his eyes were still feverishly bright when he leant across to urge. "Sara, let's get out of here, we must go where we can talk!"

"But that's not possible. I have work to do, I can't just walk out on my job, surely you realize that?"

He snapped his fingers to show his contempt of her work, then jumped to his feet and ordered, "Please go and get your wrap. If you insist, I will arrange that you are given permission to have the rest of the evening off, but it is not really necessary as you will realize when I have talked to you. Hurry now, I expect to see you in the foyer in five minutes."

Without resenting his arbitrary manner, she found herself hurrying to do his bidding. Centuries of aristocratic lineage lay behind the arrogance which in his cousin Felipe was ever-present and therefore insupportable, but which in Alvaro was rather endearing and not in the least offensive. She was not really surprised when she reached the foyer to find he had with him an affable director who was waiting to assure her that she had his permission to absent herself for the rest of the evening. With a speed that left her breathless, she was then ushered into Alvaro's car and driven at breakneck haste towards some unspecified destination.

He did not speak until the town was far beneath them, hundreds of feet below where he brought the car to rest on a steep hill looking down and across the Straits to Spain. Below, dozens of different coloured lights twinkled from a miscellany of shipping crowding the harbour, while above, huge stars encircled a sickle of pale gold moon that rested against a backcloth of midnight blue sky. Silence surrounded them, a silence she made no effort to break when she sensed his careful searching for words with which to explain his extraordinary actions. She watched him nibble his thumb, seemingly engrossed in his thoughts to the exclusion of herself, until finally curiosity overwhelmed her and she gave him a verbal prod.

"I'm waiting for an explanation, Alvaro. Why have you brought me here, and what is it you have to discuss with me that is so important that I suspect I've almost jeopardized my job to hear it?"

"Job?" he questioned vaguely, then with a wave of his hand he dismissed the subject as being of no importance.

"Well, really!" she began indignantly, "you might not think it important, but I certainly do! Do you realize . . ."

"Would you consider working for me?" he interrupted.

"Doing what?" she asked, breathless with surprise.

His voice was full of suppressed excitement when he raced out the words. "Something far more congenial than the work you are doing now and much less strenuous. You suggested the idea to me yourself when we were talking in the club earlier, and the more I think of it the more convinced I am that it is the solution I have been searching for. I know my idea is unconventional, but I hope you will not think it insulting because it is certainly not intended to be. Look, Sara, we both know my cousin Felipe has formed a totally wrong impression of you and I've thought of a way of making him suffer for his damnable tendency to jump to conclusions. I want you to agree to pose as my fiancée for a short while – a few weeks should be long enough to convince him that I mean business and that I no longer intend to allow him to make all my decisions. I will *not* be told whom I shall marry," his fist thumped into the palm of his hand with a force that jarred, "and if I can introduce you to Felipe as my future bride he will have no option but to concede defeat and to send that infant he has brought here to either approve or disapprove of myself as a suitable husband back to where she came from!"

Sara, who was fighting a losing battle against surprise and astonishment, marshalled her senses into sufficient order to ask, "You mean you've never even met this girl he wants you to marry, she's so much a stranger you don't even know her name?"

He shrugged and answered sulkily, "Her name is Isabella Savedra. She is distinctly connected – a sixth or seventh cousin, I'm not sure, and I care even less. We played together as children," he frowned at the memory, "but as far as I am concerned she could not be more of a stranger. My mother and Felipe have arranged it all between them and even though I have stated firmly and irrevocably that I will have nothing whatsoever to do with her they refuse to listen. Felipe is determined, and my great fear is that his persistence will one day wear me down until I finally find myself bound in marriage to a total stranger." He whipped round, full of urgency. "Say you will help me to fight Felipe! Please, Sara, you are my only hope, don't let me down!"

For long seconds her horror-filled eyes were held by his fixed gaze as he silently pleaded with her not to reject his idea. Her mind seethed in an agony of indecision; she dared not allow her thoughts to dwell too long upon Felipe de Panza lest the surge of bitter feeling his memory engendered should overrule the Christian beliefs nurtured within her from childhood. It was wrong to hate, wrong to desire revenge, wrong to plan the downfall even of an enemy – but the appalling truth was that, wrong or not, she *did* hate, she *did* desire to see the pride of her grandfather's executioner ground into the dust! Beads of sweat formed on her brow as she struggled to reach a decision. Never before had the forces of evil beaten so strongly within her, it was as if the devil himself mocked her puny efforts to retain sanity and his downfall was brought about only because she envisaged his face as a replica of Felipe de Panza's. In her fevered imaginings she saw his dark, satanic face laughing his contempt of her scruples and the will to submit was overcome only by forcing herself to admit that hate is self-destructive and that to succumb to it would be to afford him yet another victory. It was a relief to gasp out,

"No, Alvaro, I'm sorry, I can't do it! "

The light died out of his eyes as he sank back against his seat, bitterly disappointed. "I don't see why not," he muttered, his bottom lip protruding in a childlike pout. "It can't be that you have any regard for Felipe – he treated you and your grandfather abominably. Not that he knew the Colonel was your grandfather," he admitted carelessly.

"What do you mean?" she questioned sharply.

He looked uncomfortable for a moment, then blurted out. "From a reference he once made to yourself and your *travelling companion* I assumed he knew nothing of your relationship with the Colonel and, that being so, he had as usual put the worst possible construction upon your close association."

Her heart was thumping so hard she felt a sickening pain, but no trace of it showed in her tone when she stated. "Your cousin's opinion of me is even worse than I had thought. He has accused me openly of being a thief and a cardsharper, he has silently condemned me as a mercenery adventuress and now," her voice cracked on a forced laugh, "now you tell me he even doubts my virtue! Oh, Alvaro," she began to laugh wildly, "how funny, how very, very funny!"

He was completely out of his depth, as much bewildered by her laughter as he was by the flood of tears that followed, and all he could think of doing was cradle her trembling body until her sobbing was spent and she lay silent and still in his arms. He was astonished that the information he had disclosed, primarily to make her angry, should have had such a devastating effect, and while the silence lengthened he was forming belated apologies for his clumsiness.

But the need to apologize was forgotten when she spoke against his shoulder. "I've changed my mind, Alvaro, I'd like to take up your offer." She felt his surprised jerk, but allowed him no more than a gasp before carrying on. "But there is a condition . . ."

"Yes? Anything . . ." he urged.

Her face was still pressed against his shoulder, muffling her voice, but he was conscious of great stress when she formed the words.

"Gramps is dead. Before I do as you ask, I must have your promise never to speak of him to your cousin, neither to mention his death nor to disclose his relationship to myself. Do you agree?"

He fought down shocked remorse to make the ragged reply. "I'm terribly sorry, Sara. Of course I will never speak of him, and especially not to Felipe, I give you my word."

The villa, with its white marble floors, terraces, and swimming pool shimmering in the sun, had the appearance and ambience of a Moorish pavilion. The focal point of the house was the terrace room where a large white leather and wood seat took up most of the space in the centre and stools and loungers with scatterings of gaily-coloured cushions beckoned relaxing guests to gather like butterflies to blossoms.

Sara had caught a quick glimpse of activity around the turquoise waters of the pool before Alvaro ushered her into the more formal room where she now waited to be presented, as his fiancée, to the head of his family. To ease her nervousness, she wandered around the room supposedly examining the many beautiful pictures that hung around its walls, but in reality seeing nothing at all. Blind panic grew with every second of Alvaro's absence as she began picturing in her mind the confrontation with Felipe which he had insisted had to take place that day.

She ran nervous fingers across the gold velvet covering of a settee that ran the full length of two walls, then hastily erased with the palm of her hand the trail of fingermarks she had left on the soft material. An enormous fringed carpet deadened her footsteps as she moved restlessly towards a marble table holding a Moorish lamp delicately traced in metal, squired by two gold candlesticks containing virgin white candles. The carpet came to an abrupt end just before she reached her objective, and the loud staccato beat of her heels against the marble-tiled floor was so unexpected the sound set her heart racing. Her knees were shaking so much she sank down on to a large soft pouffe, only to jump up again at the thought that it might not be such an advantageous position in which to begin a formal meeting.

She smoothed her dress, fretting at Alvaro's extended absence. The smell of orange blossom coming from a tree outside the open window was overpowering and for one dreadful moment she felt certain she was going to be sick. Her hands were pressed to her fluttering stomach when the door was suddenly thrown open, and when her green eyes, enormous in a pale face, met those of Felipe de Panza she felt immediately and paralysingly afraid. For a split second as they faced one another no holds were barred, his look, glowering dark with contempt, took in every detail of her appearance – the delicate green cloud of dress that caught a slight draught from the open door and clung to her slender curves as if deliberately flouting their perfection before eyes determined to find fault, the smooth tanned flesh of her arms, bare except for a gold slave bangle snapped around her wrist to emphasise fragile hands and slender gold-tipped fingernails, and her darkly gleaming waterfall of hair with its highlights like trapped stars.

He had been swimming. His hair was tousled, rubbed through with a hasty towel, so that the dark glistening spirals falling across his brow afforded his usually suave features an aura of carefree vitality. But the contrasting fury in his eyes and in his tightly compressed mouth told her that he had already spoken to Alvaro and that the news he had been given had left him feeling anything but carefree. She braced herself against attack. Their confrontations had been few, but each had held an element of battle, a battle that now threatened to escalate into a full-scale war from which she sensed she would emerge with scars even greater than those she had suffered in earlier skirmishes.

Her grandfather had always maintained that attack was the finest form of defence, so with an aplomb that inwardly amazed her she directed him a cool smile and mocked sweetly, "I see Alvaro has acquainted you with our news. Have you come to offer your good wishes for our future happiness?"

His answering retort would have annihilated her completely if it had been allowed to be voiced, but even as a quickly indrawn breath hissed between his teeth preparatory, she had no doubt, to delivering a blistering tirade, a young breathless voice spoke from somewhere behind him.

"Oh, there you are, Felipe! We were wondering where you had disappeared to. Alvaro has arrived, did you know?" When the slim figure of a girl dressed in a towelling robe only partially covering a one-piece bathing suit stepped into view Sara knew instinctively that she was looking at Isabel Savedra. She was a ripe, luscious beauty with lovely flashing eyes and Titian hair and she projected the unconscious, almost puritanical sex appeal so often possessed by nubile Spanish girls. She was also shy, as was revealed when her footsteps faltered to a halt and her cheeks flooded a becoming shade of pink at the sight of Sara.

"Forgive me if I intrude, Felipe," she stumbled, her eyes downcast. "I did not know you were not alone."

Sara, however unwillingly, had to admire his superb self-control. With complete mastery, he banished the anger from his face and took hold of Isabel's hand to draw her forward into the room. "Isabel, let me introduce you to Miss Battle – Sara," he amended quickly, then, with a hard look towards her, he stressed, "A *family* friend." His look dared her to deny his assertion, dared her to disillusion the shy young girl whose voice had trilled with delight when voicing Alvaro's name, and so, although hating to allow him even one small victory, she found herself smiling agreement as she stepped forward to shake the hand Isabel immediately held out towards her.

"How do you do, Sara. Won't you come outside and join us around the pool?" she coaxed, with a quick glance at Felipe. He was forced to second the invitation or seem churlish, and Sara felt she had the advantage when, with stiff politeness, he bowed to the inevitable.

"Yes, certainly you must join us. You are no doubt anxious to meet Alvaro's mother and she, in turn, would never forgive me if I allowed you to go without an introduction."

The quick flickering of her eyelashes told him she was disconcerted, and the knowledge seemed to afford him much satisfaction. Alvaro had made no mention of his mother's presence at the villa, she was prepared to meet only one adversary, Felipe, whose forceful personality was ample strain without the added burden of a possessive mother. But her discomfiture was only momentary, she had pledged herself to help Alvaro extricate himself from his family's bondage and the sympathy and indignation she felt on his behalf gave her the courage she so badly needed to face further opposition. So she tipped up her chin and met his sardonic smile with outward nonchalance before stepping past him to follow Isabel, who was already leading the way.

"One moment, *señorita*," he checked her hurrying footsteps. "Before we proceed I must warn you, as I have already warned Alvaro, there must be no mention of your supposed engagement before I have had time to prepare my aunt for the announcement. Because of his usual lack of consideration, my cousin has had to be reminded that his mother's health has been causing us much worry. He knows, but has chosen to ignore, that her doctor has ordered complete rest and freedom from stress if her tired heart is to last out another year. At the moment she is happy, convinced her son is at last ready to settle down with the girl she expects him to marry – Isabel – and I intend to see to it that she stays happy, at least until her strength has been sufficiently built up to allow her to cope with the changed situation."

His words caught her heart with the sting of a lash, their underlying threat unmistakable. "And how do you propose to do that?" she tilted, defiantly determined to oppose what she was convinced was no more than emotional blackmail, a ploy he had thought up on the spur of the moment in an effort to baulk Alvaro's bid for freedom.

"There is no time to discuss ways and means," he rapped as Isabel's voice called out to them. "Just bear in mind that if you do not do as I direct both Alvaro and yourself will be very, very sorry! "

Her cheeks were still wildly flushed when they finally reached the small group that sat lazily around the cool blue-green waters of the pool. To her surprise Alvaro was one of them. When she appeared Isabel jumped to her feet and leant down to whisper in the ear of the white-haired old lady whose chair was next to hers. She looked up, removed her sunglasses, and extended her hand towards the somewhat timidly advancing Sara.

Ready as she was to meet unfriendliness, even cold hostility, Sara was completely taken aback when Al-

varo's mother smiled a welcome which was undoubt-
edly genuine. "My dear," the eyes shaded by a mantilla
of fine black lace were kind, "Isabel has just whispered
to me that I am about to meet a very special friend of
the family. As I know Alvaro has no time at the moment for anyone but Isabel, I have gladly guessed that
the one it is who holds you so dear to his heart is my
nephew Felipe." She cast a roguish glance around their
astonished faces. "Why you all persist in treating me
like a decrepit imbecile when you know how impossible
I am to deceive I do not know! Sara, my dear – I may
call you that, may I not? – will you please side with
me against my incorrigible family and help me to convince them that far from inflicting harm upon my stupid old heart, the good news that my dear Felipe has at
last been persuaded to part with his affection is a tonic
I have long been waiting for.

"Come, kiss me, my dear," she proffered a smooth
cheek, "then sit by me so that we may talk. I must
have all the answers ready for Felipe's mother when I
return to Spain or else be prepared to suffer her displeasure."

In various stages of shock, they all moved automat-
ically into position. Sara threw one stunned glance towards Alvaro as he placed her chair next to his mother's,
but his eyes slewed away with embarrassment and she
had no choice but to accept the seat which, mercifully,
was placed so that all she could see of Felipe was his
rigid back and the shadow of his grimly etched profile.

Isabel moved a stool next to Alvaro's chair which was placed overlooking the glistening water, isolating them both on an island of solitude he was either too loath or too cowardly to abandon. Sara's fury at being placed in such an invidious position knew no bounds. Obviously, there had been a ring of truth in Felipe's assertion that his aunt was not in good health, but Doña Maria, as she had been introduced by Isabel, was a matriarch figure, a pampered old lady whose every whim had been allowed . . . up until now!

Felipe must have sensed her objective even as the thought was formed. As her lips opened to disabuse Alvaro's mother of her hastily formed conclusions he jumped to his feet to reach her side before the first defiant word could be spoken.

"Would you like to swim, *amiga*?" he asked, his hand digging so cruelly into the soft flesh of her shoulder she all but cried out with pain.

"Oh, but, Felipe . . . !" Doña Maria moued.

"You will have plenty of time to get to know, Sara, Tia," he flashed her a white-toothed smile, "but later, when the sun is not so hot. Once you get into your stride your questions tend to develop on the lines of the Inquisition and I want Sara to try out the pool. So, to please me, will you try now to sleep, then this evening when you are more rested I promise I shall let you have her to yourself for as long as you wish." He bent over Sara with a tight set smile. "Are you agreeable, *chica*?"

She could not answer, her bottom lip was caught between her teeth biting back the pain his fingers were inflicting upon her tender flesh and so she nodded and gasped out: "Of course!" Feeling his merciless grip relax was a relief so great she could have fainted.

"Good, then that is settled," he straightened and returned his aunt's smile of agreement as he urged Sara to her feet. "Isabel has plenty of spare costumes, so if you'll follow me I'll show you where you can change."

The water felt blessedly cool against her fiery body when she slid into the pool dressed in a borrowed swimsuit of frosted pink which superbly set off the darkness of her hair and the gold tan that she had acquired in her sunny days of cruising. She was so humiliated, so full of suppressed rage she would not have been surprised to feel the water sizzle around her suffused body. She cleaved the water with smooth, clean strokes, rejoicing at its satin caress against her flushed face, and surrendered for the moment to the sheer bliss of uncomplicated solitude. She had to think, to plan, and to reorganize her opinions about Alvaro whose spineless acceptance of his cousin's dictates had left her feeling terribly vulnerable. He would have to be discounted as an ally; though full of confidence the previous evening when outlining his ideas, once within his cousin's influence he became as wax in his hands. But she must carry out the plan he had originated. Alvaro needed to be protected from himself, even more so now that she knew the full extent of Felipe's dominance over his weak-willed young cousin.

She rolled over on her back. Closing her eyes against the sun's glare, she allowed herself to float along, paddling now and then with her hands to project her body languidly through the water. She was lost in the enjoyment of the moment, her troubles almost forgotten, when a turbulence around her set the water heaving and a second later Felipe's voice commanded,

"Swim with me to the far end of the pool where we will not be overheard. I want to talk to you!"

Reluctantly, she abandoned her state of happy euphoria and followed in his wake. She would have headed towards the steps rather than seek his assistance, but he reached the side long before she did and she could not evade the hand that reached out to pull her out of the water and on to a sunbathing raft placed at the pool's edge. He stretched out on the raft like a great cat, his muscles rippling with panther-like power as he adjusted his body to a comfortable position. She was very conscious of his bare brown limbs and of the breadth of his shoulders; their strength was indication that, if he wished, he might break her own slight body in two without exerting himself in the slightest.

To occupy her hands and to keep her eyes from straying towards his uncovered limbs, she flung off her pink cap and loosened her hair from its constricting pins so that it cascaded around her bent head, screening him from her sight but also hiding her own flushed cheeks from his keen eyes. She had no idea why she should feel so burnt up with shyness. On the sun deck aboard ship she had often been surrounded by men in various stages of undress and Marc, too, had many times swum with her wearing the same kind of black swimming briefs favoured by the *señor*, but somehow none of the others had projected the primitive aura she sensed around the dark Spaniard. In shedding his clothes he had also shed the veneer of culture that had made her feel able to oppose him. In his case, clothes had not merely made the man – they had helped to cloak the sheer animal virility beneath their surface. A quick breath caught in her throat: how had she even dared to contemplate contesting the will of this man whose victory was sure to be as swift and as merciless as his retribution? She swept the curtain of hair back from her face and forced herself to meet his cynical eyes. Cowardice had won; she intended to back out, to assure him she would leave his house immediately. But then fate decided otherwise.

"Well, Señorita Battle," he forestalled her, "how much is it going to cost me to be rid of you?"

"How . . . much . . .?" she stumbled like a child grappling with new words.

"Come now," his jaw was granite hard, "spare me the preliminary games, I'm not in the mood for pretence. I wish to know what amount of money will be required to free my family from the embarrassment of your presence."

When his meaning became clear her previous decision sank without trace beneath a flood of furious anger.

"How dare you!" she whispered, her eyes mesmerized by a face as cold and unfeeling as a swaying cobra's. She felt battered by contempt when he returned with cold deliberation,

"I dare because I have previous knowledge of your methods. You do not seem to have much lasting success with the men you ensnare, *señorita*. What happened to your shipboard companion, for instance? Did he desert you, or had you no further use for him once your despicable tricks to extort money were uncovered? And the young man at the airport, what about him? You seem to have forgotten that I held in my hand evidence that he, too, had paid dearly for your favours!"

His words were missiles flung from his tongue without thought of mercy and his cold eyes did not soften when he saw how her slender body wilted beneath the weight of their bombardment. She had expected a fight, indeed she had come prepared for one, but only now did she fully realize how ill equipped she was to enter the arena with a man whose cutting tongue could reduce her spirit to ribbons with a single spate of words.

She lifted her shaking hands to her ashen face, only to have them jerked away in his hard grip.

"You haven't answered my question," he gritted. "Because of the urgency of the situation I am willing to let you name your own sum. If it were not for the fact that I am forced to consider the feelings of Alvaro's mother as well as those of his future wife I would leave him completely at your mercy. It would do the young fool good to learn his lesson the hard way, by personal experience, instead of always relying upon others to extricate him from the messes he gets himself into. You might well have been the making of Alvaro, *señorita*," he suddenly mocked. "He is still so naïve he thinks a pretty face indicates a pretty nature, but an entanglement with you would have soon disabused him of that idea! However," his mocking look disappeared with a return of grimness, "as speed is an essential essence of my plans, I must forgo that pleasure and insist that we come to an immediate agreement. How much? And do you prefer the money to be paid in cash or by cheque?"

She was quick to recognize the direction of his thoughts; if he could remove her from out of his family's orbit immediately her flying visit would soon be forgotten and her existence permanently erased from their memory. But if she stayed long enough to make friends with Doña Maria and Isabel he would run the risk of her disclosing everything to them, leaving him with some very awkward questions to answer.

She almost managed to smile when she straightened her drooping back and met his look with eyes that held newly aroused vengeance in their depths.

"I hadn't definitely decided to accept Alvaro's proposal," she told him hardly, "but you have helped me to reach a decision, *señor*. I'm not in love with your cousin, but my hatred for you goes so deep that I find myself willing to marry him simply to get even with you! So you can throw away your cheque book. As the future Señora de Leon I shall no doubt be furnished with ample money to supply my needs."

His expression evidenced the terrible passions she had aroused, and instinct forced her to her feet to flee from danger. His reaction was swift, but she managed to slip from the grip he only just managed to fasten upon her arm and dived into the water to swim faster than she had ever done in her life before towards the other end of the pool.

Half an hour later the group around the pool broke up, Doña Maria to escape the strengthening heat of the sun by seeking the coolness of her room and Isabel to go to the kitchen to inform the staff there would be two extra for dinner that evening. Of Felipe there was no sign, by the time Sara had reached the end of the pool and made haste to join the others he had disappeared from sight and had not been seen since.

Alvaro was just preparing to sidle out of view when Sara turned to speak sharply to him. "Alvaro, don't go, you must realize we have to talk!"

He shrugged. "Can't it wait until after dinner? I have some business in town that must be attended to today. I hadn't bargained on being delayed here so long. I must get back to Tangier immediately."

81

"Your business must wait!" she retorted, despising him for his attempt to avoid the awkward questions he knew she was about to ask. "But, in any case, there need be no delay in reaching Tangier, just give me a minute to change and I'll travel back with you. We can talk on the way."

He looked uncomfortable. "But we are both expected to dine here. You heard Felipe's promise to my mother, she will be most disappointed if you do not appear!"

"You needn't worry, Felipe has no intention of allowing me to stay," she broke in wryly. "No doubt he had already formed some excuse to offer your mother for my absence when he asked me how much it would cost to be rid of me immediately!"

"He asked you that?" Alvaro slowly enunciated, embarrassed colour seeping under his tan. She waited for a storm of protest on her behalf, confident that this disclosure was the prod he needed to bring out the spirit in his indolent nature, but she waited in vain. Instead of the indignant reaction she expected, all he did was drop down on to the nearest chair with a whistle of surprise and mutter helplessly: "Well, I'm damned! He said he intended being ruthless, but I'd no idea he would go that far!"

Sara's scalp prickled. "Would you mind telling me what else he had to say when you told him of our engagement?"

With a resigned shrug he settled back in his chair

and struggled to find less offensive words than those his cousin had used to convey his displeasure. "First, he threatened my complete destitution by saying he would throw me out of the family business, and after that he tried appealing to my sense of responsibility. It was my duty, he said, to marry Isabel as everyone expected it and both my mother's heart and hers would be broken if I refused to comply. When I remained adamantly opposed to the idea, he proceeded to outline in detail the many reasons why I should not become entangled – his words – with you. For a man who has met you only infrequently he has a surprising knowledge of your movements since you left the ship. Not only does he know about your job as a croupier at the Club Aziz, he knows also of your association with a man named Marc Rochefort who, according to him, has reason to regret ever having met you."

He slewed a quick glance over her set face and when she did not interrupt he carried on reluctantly, "Finally, when everything else had failed, he reminded me that my mother's health would be jeopardized by any sudden shock, such as she might receive if I acquainted her of my decision to marry you." With a shamefaced look, he leant forward to plead, "Sara, I swear that up until then I did not know the seriousness of her condition. When Felipe waved the doctor's report under my nose I realized it was out of the question to carry on with our plan. My mother can be stern at times, she often treats me like a child whose actions must always

be vetted, but I love her dearly and could never do anything to harm her. That is why," he sighed, "I have
decided to do as they ask – to marry Isabel. I could not
live with myself if any action of mine were to bring
about the death of my mother."

He was genuinely worried, and she could not find it
in her heart to condemn him. But it hurt, the fact that
her proud boast to Felipe had been so much hot air.
How he would gloat when he found out . . .

"Alvaro!" She spoke so suddenly he jerked to attention. "Felipe can't be aware of your change of mind or
he wouldn't have attempted to bribe me?" When he
nodded affirmation she bounded on, "Then need he
know just yet? If only to teach him a lesson, can't we
keep him in the dark a little longer?"

He did not try to hide his dismay.

"But why, Sara? You've no idea what he is like when
opposed, and already he's sworn to go to any lengths
to break things up between us. He means every word, I
assure you, so why tempt the devil?"

"You owe me this one favour, Alvaro! Felipe has
humiliated and threatened me and in the cause of justice I mean to see that his actions do not go unpunished.
Neither Isabel nor your mother need ever know," she
coaxed. "It will be our secret, yours and mine."

His nervous fingers sought out his cigarette case, but
when it was found he did not attempt to open it but
merely drummed a nervous tattoo upon its surface as
he tried not to become wooed over by her impassioned

84

reasoning. Even as he hesitated, her sensitive mouth began to tremble and he knew then that he was beaten.

"Very well, you win," he sighed. "I'll say nothing to Felipe about my change of plan, but I warn you, Sara, you will be dicing with danger. My mother's hastily formed conclusion that you and he are more than friends puts you both in an untenable position – one Felipe will resent. If you insist upon driving him into a corner you will have no one but yourself to blame if you find the outcome unfavourable!"

They left the villa a short while later. Sara wanted to change for dinner, so Alvaro dropped her off at the *pension* with the promise that as soon as his business was concluded he would return to drive them both back to the villa in ample time for dinner.

Her hands trembled as she ransacked her wardrobe, seeking an extra special dress with appeal enough to help her get through the difficult evening ahead. But nothing inspiring came to light, so she unlocked the two large cabin trunks that were stacked, still unpacked, in a closet and continued searching. One dress after another was discarded as she burrowed through the collection of fabulous clothes that constituted the only profit accrued from her partnership with her grandfather. At last, she emerged satisfied, clutching one of her more recent purchases, a culotte fashioned out of finest nylon jersey, so insubstantial it rippled like a silken breeze through her fingers. Holding it against her body, she stepped eagerly towards the mirror and

85

stared with satisfaction at the effects its multi-coloured greens, blues and golds had upon her raven hair and wide expectant eyes. "My choice of ammunition might not be as obvious as yours, *señor*," she murmured softly, "but let's hope it will prove to be just as deadly!" She dared not dwell too long on her plan of revenge; the idea had been formulated not from conceit, but from the many advances she had received from men over the past few years. Men found her attractive, and Felipe de Panza was a man. It must therefore follow, she reasoned, that if she were in a position to bombard him with the wiles that came naturally to every woman, sooner or later a crack must show in his defences. She would work on him, subtly but intently, until he was completely disarmed, and then, when the moment was right, she would shatter his enormous self-esteem by laughing in his face! Just to think about it made her tremble with frightened anticipation, but she felt she was committed and there could be no turning back. As Alvaro's fiancée she was bound to see a lot of Felipe and so long as Alvaro kept his promise not to divulge his change of plan she could safely count on having ample time to ensure his cousin's downfall.

Alvaro picked her up as promised and they reached the villa with time to spare. He took her into a small salon and after supplying her with a drink and assuring her that she would soon be joined by the rest of the family, he excused himself and went up to his room to change. The windows of the salon opened out on to the garden, so she put down her glass and stepped outside to experience at close quarters the eternal marvel of the orange tree bearing ripe fruit and blossom at the same time. She sniffed deeply, revelling in the sweet, sharp tang, and leant forward to caress with an inquisitive finger the white, star-shaped blossoms that clung around the richly coloured globules of fruit.

"Good evening, *señorita!*" Even as the words shattered the evening calm a pair of hard hands clamped her waist and spun her round without thought of gentleness to face the *señor's* hard eyes.

"Let me go!" She fought him with instinctive resentment, his attack catching her completely off guard.

"Not until we finish the discussion you so abruptly terminated this afternoon," he suavely refused. "You were too quick for me then, but even if you should fight all night you will not be allowed to escape me this time." He pulled her forward and demanded with a steely glint, "Are you going to be sensible, or must I continue to employ brute force?"

"What other kind would you know of?" she spat furiously.

His amused laugh clashed with the thinly veiled dislike in his voice. "Am I to infer from that remark that you consider me a brute?" He lowered his head and sent a chill of fear through her by menacing softly, "You underestimate me, *señorita!*"

"No doubt!" She flung away from him and he allowed her to go, but his wary look was proof that he was ready to pounce if she should make the effort necessary. She heard the snap of his cigarette case and saw a flare of light in the dusk before he spoke again.

"Do you still insist upon carrying on with your mockery of an engagement to Alvaro, even though you know the pain it will cause his mother and Isabel?"

She swallowed hard. His presence was so dominating, the wide sweep of his shoulders under a white dinner jacket was intimidating and his pristine linen was a foil that threw into relief the granite hardness of his profile. "We ... we have decided, Alvaro and I," she stammered, "to keep our engagement a secret for the time being as we are in no hurry to get married. In the meantime, I intend to become better acquainted with Doña Maria so that when we do actually decide upon a date she will perhaps have begun to like me enough to consider me acceptable as a daughter-in-law."

"*Santa Virgen!*" he hissed, his dark eyes flaming. "Have you no shame? I did not imagine that even you would contemplate carrying out such a deception against a frail old lady and an unsophisticated child! As for Alvaro, I must suppose the poor fool is so much in love he will agree to anything!" Further tumultuous words were crushed even as the cigarette he discarded was crushed beneath his foot. Exercising supreme control, his voice dangerously low, he asked, "Do you realize, I wonder, that I have it in my power to deprive Alvaro of the very substantial income he now enjoys? He holds a very junior position in our firm. One word from me and you could find yourself engaged to a pauper!"

"But wouldn't you then be defeating your own ends?" she enquired sweetly, experiencing for the first time a heady taste of power. "If you should be tempted to carry out such a threat would not the shock inflicted upon your aunt be greater than any she might be in danger of receiving from me?" She laughed up into his angry face and taunted, "You are out-manoeuvred, *señor*, so why don't you act as a gentleman should and admit to an honourable defeat?"

During dinner she made sure her eyes strayed as little as possible in his direction as he sat smouldering at the head of the table. She was not finished with him by any means, but she needed a breathing space in which to marshal her exultant thoughts and to muster her forces for the second attack that had to be timed to a nicety if the element of surprise that was its main ingredient was to inflict the maximum of damage. None of them guessed, as they proceeded through each delicious course with relaxed enjoyment, that her mind was seething with activity, weighing up each remark that was addressed to her, just waiting the opportunity of an opening which would allow her to show her hand with maximum effect. Unwittingly, it was Doña Maria who paved the way when, with the persistence of the aged, she returned to the subject of Felipe and his supposed attachment. She spooned up the last of her *Zabaglione*, obviously relishing the delicate blending of chilled whipped cream and rich Marsala wine, then pushed away her glass with a satisfied sigh before questioning Sara,

"When did Felipe and yourself become acquainted, my dear? Was it recently, or has the rascal been keeping you to himself for some time?"

Sara knew without having to look in his direction that Felipe's head jerked suddenly erect and the conversation between himself and Isabel ceased abruptly while he waited to hear her reply. This was the chance she had been waiting for and she took it, though not without experiencing a thrill of exhilarating terror. Doña Maria was completely charmed by the rosy blush, downcast eyes and shy whisper that seemed to indicate to all those watching the confused happiness of a girl in love.

"I feel I have known Felipe all my life," she cooed with wicked enjoyment, "but in actual fact we met on the *African Queen* only a few short weeks ago."

"And it was love at first sight for both of you!" Doña Maria clapped with delight, completely carried away by the play upon her emotions. Sara chanced a swift glance towards Felipe and a surge of triumph drowned the inward fear she felt at the thought of his retaliation, but anything was worth enduring for the pleasure of seeing him so completely disconcerted. He had insisted upon her playing out the farce that afternoon, confident that by evening she would be gone, now he was hoist by his own petard and she was gaining great satisfaction from watching him writhe . . .

"Felipe, dare I ask, or am I being rather premature?" Doña Maria hesitated, flags of excited colour in her cheeks, then rushed on, "When is the wedding to be?"

Sara felt she had been struck in the solar plexus. Events were moving too rapidly, she had intended only to annoy Felipe not to trap him – that might turn out to be altogether too dangerous a manoeuvre!

Only Alvaro seemed to read correctly Felipe's set expression. Sending Sara a quick glance of warning, he attempted to smooth things over by reprimanding his mother. "Shame upon your curiosity, Mother! What Sara must be thinking of your prying I hardly dare to imagine."

His mother's face crumpled like a chastened child's at his uncustomary severity, leaving him feeling a complete moron. But even as his shoulders lifted in a masculine shrug of helplessness, Felipe's deliberately amused voice broke the strained silence.

"Why all the fuss?" he demanded, one dark eyebrow lifted quizzically. "You, Tia, shall have your answers as soon as I know them myself, whereas you, Alvaro," he turned on him with a meaning glint, "can safely leave Sara's feelings to me."

Sara gasped. The gauntlet was thrown down with a vengeance! Obviously Felipe was taking Alvaro's interference as a sign of jealousy and fear that he might betray the truth was forcing him to accept the need to act out the lie. She was left no time to wonder further. Felipe's hand burned through the flimsy material of her sleeve as he grasped her arm and began propelling her in the direction of the garden. Without giving her time to protest, he made their excuses.

"I am sure you will understand if Sara and I do not join you for coffee. I have much to say to her and the words will come much more easily in the garden. Don't you agree, *cara*?" he hissed in her ear.

Doña Maria's face brightened when a lovely rush of colour stained Sara's cheeks, and when she noted how incapable she seemed of tearing her eyes from the smile that twisted Felipe's mouth into lines of almost sardonic humour.

"Of course, of course!" she beamed.

Alvaro's reaction was to emit a harsh sound that died in his throat as soon as it was born and which to Sara sounded like a croak of commiseration.

She was marched without ceremony out of earshot. Prickles of sweat began to form on her brow, but she held her head erect as he piloted her in grim silence along the dark paths. It was only when he jerked to a halt and rasped out: "Now, tell me exactly what it is you are trying to achieve!" that her nerve went and she was left speechless looking up into his furious eyes.

He was so big, so dark, and so tight-lipped with anger that her mind refused to advance beyond those facts. Even when he shook her impatiently, as if he would rattle loose the words from her tongue, she continued to infuriate him by remaining mute. As the silence lengthened she tried desperately to release her paralysed vocal cords, but the words simply would not come. With an exasperated sigh he shook her again and as he did so his elbow caught the branches of an orange tree, dislodging blossoms that rained upon her bent head like a shower of tiny white stars.

He speared down at her and the sight of her mutely appealing face with its rich coronet of blossom spangled hair seemed to goad him further. With a sudden rough movement he tilted her chin. "Perhaps I've been a fool," he muttered through clenched teeth. "Is this what you are waiting for?" His hard mouth descended upon lips still partly open and for infinite hateful moments she was tortured by a kiss that spelled out far more effectively than words ever could the contempt she held in his eyes. He punished her thoroughly and cold-bloodedly until she was reduced to a helpless puppet in his arms. When finally he pushed her away, she staggered back until she felt the welcome solidarity of a tree trunk which offered her trembling body the support her limbs refused to supply. For long seconds she clung to it, even less capable of speech than she had been before his onslaught, and waited for the condemnation she was certain was to follow. But he, too, seemed to be labouring under some kind of strain; his compressed mouth, his outthrust jaw, and the fathomless darkness of his eyes all suggested furiously leashed anger, anger that was directed inwardly – *against himself*!

Relief surged through her veins like some instant

acting drug, relaxing her taut nerves and calming her mind's tumultuous clamouring so that she was again able to think. She had *not* imagined an infinitesimal hint of tenderness creeping in unawares at the end of that punishing kiss! His final rejection had been too swift, too hastily accomplished for a man who was supposed to be in complete control of his emotions! A shuddering sigh escaped her; right from the beginning she had suspected that her impulsive plan was doomed to failure, that its outcome would be ignominious defeat, but now. . .! Could it possibly be that the mighty Don's defences really *were* in danger of being breached?

CHAPTER V

FOR days afterwards a small enigmatic smile tugged at the corner of Sara's mouth, exciting the curiosity of all who saw it. She was certain that nothing could now go wrong, every move she made was destined to succeed. Doña Maria had again proved her worth as an ally, insisting she should move into the villa for the duration of her own stay, and Sara, though flying in the face of her host's unspoken disapproval, had quickly agreed.

But three days had gone by without her having had a chance to further her plans. She had spent her time chatting with Doña Maria and swimming with Isabel, trying to make up to them both for the absence of Alvaro, who had been ordered back to work at the plantation. Felipe, she had seen only at dinner each evening, when his cool calculating eyes and set features had given lie to the hopes she had nurtured since their last encounter. However, the fact that he was so obviously avoiding her gave some substance to her theory that he was not entirely immune to her presence, so she was content to bide her time, confident that within the relatively small confines of the villa he could not avoid her indefinitely.

A voice intruded upon her train of thought. They

were sitting on the terrace overlooking the pool, Doña Maria gently dozing in a chair placed between Sara's and Isabel's, when the younger girl stirred impatiently, then pouted, "I still do not understand why Felipe found it necessary to send Alvaro away. Surely the men employed in the vineyards are capable of carrying out their work without supervision? I think it mean of Felipe, I really do!"

"Someone has to give orders, child," Doña Maria opened sleepy eyes to reprove mildly. "Our estates are large and widely scattered, it is too much to expect Felipe to continue to carry the full burden alone. He was a mere boy when he took over the running of the business – much younger than Alvaro is now – but he did not hesitate to give up his pleasures when his father and my own dear husband died almost within a year of each other, and he has managed alone ever since. It is time he was allowed to relax and now that Alvaro has finally agreed to do his share I look forward to seeing Felipe recoup his lost years." She smiled across at Sara. "And with you to help him, my dear, I'm sure he will. Felipe as a young man was always so carefree and *vital*. I envy you the pleasure of his company when his youthful spirits are regained."

An image of Felipe's disapproving, aloof face flashed before Sara's eyes and it was with the utmost difficulty that she tried to imagine his grim features cast into a mould of gay abandon. Responsibilities had dampened any flair for enjoyment that might have existed in the younger Felipe; the fetters accepted willingly by the boy would be relinquished reluctantly by the man whose back had become accustomed to their weight.

Isabel's shrug conveyed all the selfishness of impatient youth. "But why so far away?" she wailed. "There are other vineyards nearer than those on the slopes of the Rif mountains. If Felipe had deliberately contrived to get rid of Alvaro he couldn't have found a more desolate place of banishment. There are no towns near at hand, no means of communication other than by messenger, and absolutely no civilized people for miles around – just wild, barbaric Rifs and their families. Felipe is a heartless villain to expect Alvaro to exist in such desolation!"

She was obviously echoing Alvaro's own words, his dismay upon being told where he was to spend the next few weeks had been displayed for all to see and sharp words had been exchanged between himself and Felipe before he had reluctantly driven off with the threat that should he find it too unbearable he intended to return immediately. If Felipe were not so obsessed with the idea of removing Alvaro from her own vicinity, Sara chuckled with inward amusement, Alvaro's recent lack of resistance to the plan to marry him off to Isabel might have registered, but as it was his blind stubbornness was hindering his own plans.

Isabel sensed her amusement and was provoked by it. "I think it very unkind of you to regard my troubles

so lightly, Sara," she rebuked with offended dignity.
"You who are lucky enough to have your fiancé near
to hand ought to be able to spare a little sympathy for
those less fortunate."

Sara reacted with an immediate apology. "I'm so
sorry, Isabel. Please don't think me unsympathetic. I
feel very deeply about your separation from Alvaro
and would do anything in my power to help, surely you
know that?"

Mollified, Isabel shrugged, then permitted herself a
wan smile. "You have a right to feel happy. It is I who
should feel ashamed of the jealousy that causes me to
begrudge you the joy I cannot have myself. But I do
miss Alvaro so!" She sighed, then seemed to drift away
on a tide of memory with a dreamy soulful look. Doña
Maria exchanged a conspiratorial grin with Sara. Isabel's nature was as volatile as any of her race, one minute soaring to the heights, the next scouring the depths,
but she bore no malice and Sara found Doña Maria's
fondness for Isabel echoed in her own heart at each
stage of her progressing friendship with the younger
girl.

"Is the heartless villain permitted to join you, or will
my presence interrupt a further spate of confidences?"
Felipe's dry question startled them, his fleeting look of
contempt warning Sara that he had been there long
enough to overhear her exchange with Isabel. Colour
burned her cheeks. His appearance had again coincided
with circumstances disadvantageous to herself and she

knew he was notching up yet another mark against her — this time for treachery.

But her wild colour was viewed with delight by Doña Maria, and even Isabel was generous enough to remark without rancour, "It seems one of us, at least, welcomes the sight of you, Felipe. I can only wish that I too had cause to blush at the unexpected arrival of one who fills my thoughts." She laughed, then relented. "But of course you may join us, *amigo*! Heartless you may be, but a villain you most certainly are not. Come, pull up a chair and sit by me so that I can pester you for news of Alvaro!"

He straightened from kissing the cheek his aunt had proffered, but refused Isabel's offer. "Much as I would like to I cannot spare more than a few minutes. I have something of importance to discuss with Sara, so if you will both excuse us while we go into the library?"

Now that the opportunity to be alone with him had arrived, Sara discovered a contrary streak that made her feel extremely reluctant to comply. "Can't we talk out here?" she offered desperately, hating the indomitable, cold look that was visible only to her.

"No, Sara," his tender smile deceived the others, but underneath his velvet tone she recognized an iron determination that would not be thwarted however much evasion she might attempt.

"The child is shy, Felipe." Doña Maria's hand reached out to comfort Sara. "Do not allow this nephew

99

of mine to deceive you, my dear. When you have known him as long as I, you will realize that the flint-like exterior he shows to the world hides a heart as vulnerable as any child's."

Sara suffered his mocking laughter as he guided her through the house in the direction of the library. She could hardly blame his aunt for her totally inaccurate summing up of his character; his split personality was so cleverly concealed he appeared as two complete entities – one a saint, the other a reincarnation of the devil. His actions had been the cause of her grandfather's death, and yet she had to make herself appear attracted to him. She prayed for strength!

But such was the intentness of his thoughts he forgot even to offer her a chair. She stood watching while he paced the book-lined room with its aroma of leather and polished wood, his brow furrowed as if the opening he sought eluded him. Finally, his tone almost casual, he addressed her. "Your plans seem to be working well. I must congratulate you." A rabbit mesmerized by a snake could not have felt more stricken. How could he possibly have found out? She had mentioned her plan to no one, so how . . .? "Not only has my aunt taken a liking to you, she is continually singing your praises." With relief she heard him follow on. "No doubt she will still be shocked to learn that you and not Isabel are to be her son's bride, but the blow will not be so severe as it would have been had a total stranger been presented as her future daughter-in-law." He moved until his towering presence blocked everything from sight and she was forced to meet eyes that were appraising her with puzzling inscrutability. "Yes, your idea was very cleverly conceived. You have managed to make fools of us all."

She made an involuntary movement of dissent, for the picture of deception he painted was distasteful, but he surprised her into silence with the resigned admission, "I was wrong to oppose your engagement to Alvaro, I see that now. Obviously, it cannot be expected of him that he should give orders to others and yet be denied the right to make his own personal decisions. Both for his sake and for the sake of the business, I am forced to acknowledge the wrong I have done him — and you. I intend to make reparation as soon as possible. Can you be ready to accompany me on the journey to the plantation early tomorrow morning? Alvaro will need a lot of convincing that I mean what I say and your presence should act as an assurance that from now on his life is his to live as he wishes, without interference of any kind from me."

The uncharacteristic surrender was so staggering she could hardly take it in. At last Alvaro was to be free! The boy was to be allowed to become a man, to act, to decide, even to love as he fancied! It was great news. Her joy on his behalf knew no bounds, and that, together with the relief she felt at her own release from an unbearable situation, was responsible for her expression of supreme happiness. No need to tell Felipe of their bogus engagement; she would leave it to Alvaro to include that explanation amongst the many others which would have to be exchanged before the two cousins reached complete understanding.

"But that's wonderful news, *señor*!" His dark, quizzical look swept her rapturous face, but he forbore to comment. "I'll be very happy to accompany you tomorrow," she babbled on, her mind completely occupied with the thought of Alvaro's reaction to the news of his release from bondage. "Isabel can help me to pack . . ."

"Isabel must not be told!" he rapped with a return of his usual arrogance.

"No, of course not, I understand perfectly." Isabel would be bound to ask a lot of awkward questions if she knew of the journey that was about to be undertaken – questions Alvaro would be best left to answer.

"Wear something suitable for travelling in an open jeep," he ordered, "and pack a warm coat to wear at night when the wind blows cooler. Be ready to leave at sunrise – and remember, not a word to Isabel or to my aunt. When Alvaro returns he will tell them himself what he plans to do."

Dawn light was barely spearing the skyline when he drove the jeep to the front of the house where she was waiting. His cursory nod somehow conveyed an unspoken approval of the serviceable cream-coloured trouser suit she was wearing and the topcoat which was slung casually around her shoulders. She clambered up beside him and without exchanging a word of greeting they set off on the journey.

She knew there were two hundred miles of Rif Mountains stretching eastwards to the Algerian border and that the whole of the area they were to travel contained barely half a dozen towns of any importance, but she was not prepared for the beauty that was gradually unfolded as they travelled along the road towards Tetouan. She feasted her eyes upon sparkling blue sea that sometimes lapped its tideless caress against the golden sands of numerous deserted beaches and sometimes against cliffs splashed with gentle colour. Gradually, the mountain's far-off appeal grew nearer and soon they were traversing green rounded ranges, full of folds and curves smoothed down and eroded by heavy rains. The roads were bad, making the ride rather uncomfortable, but she had no intention of complaining. Every now and then she had sensed a quick, amused glance from her silent companion that told her he was anticipating hearing vocal evidence of her growing discomfiture, so she gritted her teeth and vowed never to allow him that particular satisfaction.

His attitude was puzzling. For the first hour he had remained morose, his mouth set in lines of uncompromising sternness, but as the miles between themselves and the villa lengthened his humour grew, melting the ice in his eyes and dispersing the granite hardness from his jaw. It was not until she heard him humming that her suspicions were really aroused, and by that time they were many miles from civilization, travelling a long, lonely road which for all she knew might stretch into infinity.

She did not attempt to disguise the sudden fear that clutched her heart when she charged him, "I don't believe you are taking me to Alvaro! You've tricked me – told me deliberate lies to get me away from the villa!"

Her fears were confirmed when he threw back his head and laughed. "How perceptive of you, *señorita*, and how perfectly correct is your assumption. I did manoeuvre you out of the villa because your tactics there were meeting with too much success. As for Alvaro, I expect that at this very moment he is being reunited with Isabel. I received word last night that he had left the plantation and was on his way home. We would no doubt have passed him if I had not calculated correctly and taken a different route from the one he has chosen. By this time he will have arrived at the villa and been told by either his mother or by Isabel that you are accompanying me on a long-awaited holiday. How will he react to that, do you think? However much he might wish it, he will be hard tried to believe that a girl who can disappear with another man as soon as his back is turned could be genuinely in love with himself!" He pulled up at the side of the road and gave her incredulous, angry face his full attention. Satisfaction sparkled in his eyes and as he watched her fight for control he showed every sign of savouring his victory to the full.

"You . . . you fiend! You unspeakable barbarian! You're worse than the poor uncivilized wretches you employ – you at least have had the benefit of an education whereas they have the excuse of ignorance! Have you *no* scruples? Are you so self-obsessed, so much a victim of omnipotence that you think there are no rules you cannot break?" When she realized her tirade was having little effect, she lost control completely and raised her hand to strike. But with the speed of a whiplash her hand was captured and held forcefully away.

"Oh, no, *señorita*, not again!" he gritted. "Once before I suffered that indignity at your hands, but if you ever again attempt it I promise your punishment will be tailored to suit." With a swift change of mood he informed her carelessly, "Perhaps it will help to convince you that I mean what I say if I explain that I too have Rif blood in my veins. Many years ago, when Spaniards first invaded Morocco, one of my ancestors was captured and held prisoner by the Rif tribesmen. These people have always resented domination from any outside source. They fought many fierce campaigns against my own people and against the French, and even now it is not unknown for disturbances to occur in some parts of the mountains."

She blinked at the fantasy of it all, but she gave his words her complete attention. "Somehow," he went on, "this ancestor of mine infiltrated the hearts of these great, independent tribesmen and instead of being put to death he was accepted by them. In return, he showed them how to cultivate their land so as to provide sufficient food to fill stomachs that up until then had always felt hunger. He helped to nurse their sick and to educate their children, and as the years went by it was forgotten by all that he had ever been a prisoner. He married a beautiful Rif girl who gave him a son just before she died. He then returned to Spain, for his child's sake, but he made frequent journeys back to these mountains to visit his friends. That is why my family have been tolerated here all these years, *señorita*. Anyone who bears the name Panza is regarded by them as a blood brother. Have you now been sufficiently warned?"

Cold fear kept her silent as she withstood his probing stare. She believed his story implicitly. Now she could understand his uncanny likeness to the tall, haughty tribesmen who occasionally strode the streets of Tangier, their cloaks flaring behind them with all the arrogance expected of such a proud race. His face reflected the same cruelty, his eyes the same contempt, his actions were carried out with the same callous disregard of inflicted pain . . . Her throat was tight when she forced out the question,

"What do you intend doing with me?"

He recognized the echo of defeat in her question and was pleased by it. For a long moment he remained silent, seemingly savouring some devilish plan that afforded him endless pleasure, then his eyes swung towards her, bombarding her with reflected brilliance so that her heart leapt with terrified anticipation.

"I'm going to marry you, *señorita*! Only according to the Rif custom, of course, but the ceremony will serve its purpose in that even Alvaro will hesitate to bring down the wrath of the Rifs upon his head by casting desirous eyes upon one of their brother's possessions!"

For the remainder of the journey Sara sat huddled in panic-stricken silence, convinced she was in the company of a madman. Too late now to wish she had heeded Alvaro's warning, too late to even attempt an explanation to the man whose Spanish reserve and fiery Arab blood mated in his veins so uneasily and with such devastating results. Doña Maria's assessment of his character could be excused. She had seen only the Spanish Don, considerate and courteous in the bosom of his family, whereas she seemed always fated to arouse the sleeping forces of wild recklessness that were a legacy from his beautiful pagan ancestress. In the midst of civilization this strain was subdued, subjugated by the demands of society, but how much effort would he make to contain it once he was back amongst his primitive brotherhood. . .?

When vine terraces appeared in view she knew their journey was almost over. Tall men clothed in ragged cotton shirts, their legs bound with rawhide strips of leather to protect them from briars and thistles, straightened from their labours to wave an enthusiastic greeting as they passed, but not even the menial tasks that occupied them, nor the poverty of their attire, could detract one whit from the untrammelled, almost swaggering image they projected.

The village was little more than a compound containing primitive huts, their walls made of mud or stone held together with mud mortar, and roughly roofed with reeds. A stockade made up of branches of thorn bushes woven among prickly pear surrounded the whole settlement and inside its perimeter sloe-eyed children tended the beasts that supplied milk, and chickens so scrawny they seemed barely capable of supplying eggs. With horn blaring, he drove into the centre of the compound and in a matter of seconds the jeep was engulfed by a crowd of squealing, happy children all anxious to greet him. Laughing with obvious enjoyment, he allowed them to crawl over him, suffering tugged hair, sharp elbows in his ribs, and sticky hands that reduced his immaculate bush shirt to a mass of crumpled linen.

Fighting off their attentions, he grabbed the bag he had stowed in the back of the jeep and when they saw it their mouths pursed into oohs and ahs of anticipation. They scrambled down, still screaming their excitement, and lined up in an orderly row as if taking part in a well-loved ritual.

He handed Sara the bag of sweets and instructed, "Give each of them an exact amount so there will be no squabbling, but be careful of that imp at the end of the row. He is crippled and his great soulful eyes underline his misfortune, but he is actually the soul of mischief and any favour he receives will be bragged about vociferously until the other children are riled into giving him a thrashing." She glanced along the line of children until she spotted at the end a small skeleton of a boy whose left leg was so deformed he could not have stood without the stick fashioned into a crutch that was tucked under his arm. Even as she watched, he sensed her interest and turned his liquid brown eyes in her direction. A lump lodged in her throat; he looked so solitary, so very much as she felt, she wanted to run and cuddle his racked little body in her arms.

"What is his name?" she asked, her voice betraying a suspicion of a quiver.

"Khairy," he answered, then with a quirk, "and it seems the cunning little devil has achieved yet another conquest. Weak, downtrodden males seem to hold a fascination for you, *señorita*. Perhaps it is hardly surprising I do not find favour in your eyes." He wheeled away, leaving her to distribute the sweets to the impatiently waiting children.

When they had been divided equally and to everyone's satisfaction, Khairy appointed himself her guide by attaching himself to her side and offering to show her around the village. She had the choice of either accepting or being left stranded – there was no sign of the *señor* – so she answered gratefully, "Thank you, Khairy, it will be nice to have a companion who can speak English. You are a very clever boy. Who taught you?"

He swelled with importance and his face showed boundless contempt of the rest of the children when he glanced in their direction. "My mother, and she in turn was taught by my father who was killed in a battle before I was born. He was the son of a Caid, a great and wise man, but after he was killed my mother returned here to her own people. I have been brought up with these ignorant Rifs, but one day when I am a man, I will take my mother back to my grandfather's kasbah at the oasis of El Safida." This was said with such conviction she had to believe him. His broken body caged a spirit as indomitable as her own and her optimism was revived by his remarkable courage.

"I'm sure you will, Khairy," she answered softly. "Your mother is a very lucky woman to have a son such as you."

His suspicious look told her he suspected her of laughing at him, but when she met his eyes with steady earnestness his face creased into a broad smile and his hand was pushed into hers with a heartwarming gesture of friendliness. "Come with me, *señorita*, I will take you to meet my mother. She, too, grows weary of gossiping peasants and her day will be brightened if she can speak with you." She followed him to one of the huts, but when he stepped inside to lead the way she hesitated, unsure whether or not she would be welcome. She was about to turn away when Khairy reappeared holding the hand of one of the most beautiful women Sara had ever seen. She was tall with a willowy, graceful carriage, and her head, braided with glossy black hair, was carried proudly erect, giving credence to the allusions of past grandeur made by her son. Her skin had the tint and the bloom of olives and her sad, lustrous eyes spoke of mystery and pain buried too deep ever to be forgotten.

"I am Zuela, mother of Khairy," she spoke with a charming lilt. "If you will honour us with a visit you are assured of a welcome." Sara stepped inside to be confronted with appalling poverty. There was just one large room divided by curtains of grass matting. The floor was of hard beaten earth and the solitary window was merely a frame with a wooden shutter. Round three sides of the room was a shelf of earth spread with mats and rugs which were evidently used as seats by day and as covers at night. Very little daylight penetrated, and as she groped her way forward Zuela moved to light an oil lamp which cast eerie shadows as it swung backwards and forwards at her touch. Sara wondered how dignity could possibly be maintained under such circumstances, and when Zuela politely asked if she would favour them by accepting some mint tea she was filled with admiration for the woman who moved inside her pitiful hut as if it had the ambience of the princely kasbah that once had been her home.

But the tea Sara gulped down was delicious, a much longed for refreshment made of green tea, mint and sugar that was nectar to her parched throat. She nodded grateful acceptance when offered a second cup.

"The *señorita* visits with the *señor*, Mother," Khairy offered. "His visit is to last perhaps as long as a week."

"That is good news." A hint of colour ran under Zuela's olive skin, but her voice was calm when she stated, "We are always pleased to receive a visit from Don Felipe. He has done much for our people." When Sara's eyebrows elevated, Zuela gently reproved, "Please do not blame the *señor* for the poverty that surrounds us. The Rif are an independent race who react unfavourably to change. They much prefer their own ways, even though they are primitive, and the *señor*'s greatest wisdom lies in his ability to accept our manners and customs. But even so, slowly, and by exercising extreme discretion, he has managed to improve our standard of hygiene and our knowledge of working the land. Doctors pay us regular visits to check upon our health and he has even managed to persuade some of the tribesmen to undergo dental treatment, something that could never have been achieved a few years ago."

"And I am to have an operation," put in Khairy. "When I am older and stronger the *señor* is taking me to a large hospital so that my leg may be straightened, is that not so, Mother?"

This time there was no mistaking the blush that set Zuela's cheeks afire. Sara's heart gave an inexplicable jolt as with sudden insight she became aware that the mere mention of Don Felipe's name was enough to arouse in Zuela an emotion so strong it was reflected in her eyes as an unmistakable glow.

A small commotion outside heralded the arrival of a young Arab boy whose frantic gesticulations made Sara sickeningly aware that her presence was required elsewhere. When Zuela confirmed this assumption it was as much as she could do to refrain from pleading for help to escape. But the instinct was crushed under a weight of fear that Zuela herself might be made to suffer for daring to interfere in the affairs of a man so highly regarded by these unpredictable Rifs. So, as casually as she was able, she thanked Zuela and her son for their hospitality before following her impatient guide outside into unexpected darkness. Night had fallen with its usual suddenness while she was being entertained inside the hut, and its denseness, coupled with the unfamiliarity of her surroundings, made her hesitate before groping her way forward in the direction taken by her swiftly retreating guide.

"Wait! Please wait . . ." she called after him, suffering a fear of the solitary gloom that was closing in on her with silent menace. But the boy either did not heed or was deaf to her cry, because the sound of his footsteps grew gradually fainter, then faded completely. She stood stock still, shivering, her heart pounding with dull, heavy thuds. She was ashamed of her fear, a long-forgotten relic of her childhood in the orphanage where pleas for a nightlight had been frowned upon as bids for extra attention. She had thought the fear long outgrown, but her leaden limbs and dry mouth were ample evidence that the deeply buried dread had

113

needed only favourable conditions to achieve its resurrection.

A sudden deepening of the gloom in front of her brought a scream of hysteria to her lips. The shadow moved forward with a muttered imprecation, then, to her indescribable relief, spoke soothingly.

"Do not be afraid, you are quite safe."

She almost collapsed into the arms of the Arab whose tall figure clad in a voluminous *djellaba* loomed like a monster out of the darkness. Half laughing, half crying, she clung to him while his strong arms cradled her shaking body and his hand, gentle as a woman's, stroked her hair with light, soothing strokes.

"I'm sorry," she gasped finally, experiencing a strong reluctance to leave the comfort of his arms but forcing herself nevertheless to step a pace away from him. She peered upwards, trying to pierce the darkness that veiled his features, but the moonless night defended its secret, leaving her with a sense of frustrated longing.

The shadow spoke again, his voice tender but with a hint of laughter. "The night has thrown many things in my path, but never before such an enjoyable experience. Things that come out of the darkness are often cruel, or predatory, and are almost always startling, but within the boundaries of our village you need not be afraid. Tell me, what dire misfortune did you imagine was about to befall you when I appeared? Did you suppose me a ghost, a wild animal, or perhaps a predatory male – sometimes the most dangerous of all the species?"

Strangely, his amusement did not anger her. His voice was too kind, his touch too compassionate, she knew she could trust him. Whether she had felt the lack of a sympathetic listener since the death of her grandfather, or whether it was the relief of his reassuring presence that loosened her tongue she was not sure, but she surprised herself by pouring out all the feelings of terror she had felt as a child when the dormitory lights had been switched off and enormous shadow giants had spread up and along the colour-washed walls, huge distorted shapes that watched unmovingly just waiting to pounce on the first unwary child who closed his eyes.

She expected some teasing remark when she faltered to a stop, but his shadow remained still and silent. "Have I been boring you?" she laughed lightly, even though grim memories had brought beads of sweat to her brow. He moved and she felt his hands upon her shoulders. She was drawn forward until her head rested against his chest, his hard, lithe body felt taut and somehow full of anger. Silently, he rocked her in his arms until peace flowed through her veins and her tense body was calm and relaxed. She felt his lips cool and firm upon her brow as he whispered, "Gallant child, brave little warrior!" She never again wanted to move. His arms were the haven she had sought, his strength the strength she had yearned to find in the men she had known but which up until then she had never been even remotely near to finding. She struggled to tell him so, ached to find the words to describe her feelings of wonder . . .

The sound of swiftly running footsteps encroached, breaking the spell that bound her in spirit to the anonymous shadow who held her. She spun round as the boy who had previously been sent to fetch her loomed into sight and felt bereft as the arms that held her were withdrawn, leaving a warm impression where they had rested.

"All right, I'm coming," she assured the panting boy, then turned to speak again to her unknown companion. But he had gone, melted into the night as silently as he had come, without waiting even to say goodbye. A wave of desolation swept her and for seconds she struggled with an onrush of tears. But he had not completely gone, he had communicated to her a part of himself, a courage, a sense of belonging, and the wonderful satisfaction of knowing that she had at last met a man whose nature was as strong as it was gentle, a man whose very tenderness was proof of masculine assurance, the kind of man she had begun to doubt even existed. With a springing step and shining eyes she followed the boy to where she was bidden.

As she suspected, it was Felipe who had summoned her. She was led into a large, newly erected black tent decorated internally with colourfully patterned carpets, silken drapes and mounds of plump cushions – treasures hoarded by the Rif families but surrendered willingly for the comfort of their guests. Ornate lamps cast a warm pool of light into the centre of the tent, but beyond its perimeter deep shadows stretched, giving an illusion of sinister depth to the surrounding darkness. She gave a startled gasp when Felipe's voice rasped out as he stepped from out of the shadows into the pool of light.

"I trust you have been sufficiently entertained during my absence?" Her wide eyes mirrored shock as they swung in his direction. The change in him was as incredible as it was startling. A striped *djellaba*, long, loose, with wide sleeves and a hood, adapted to his lean length as no other garment could. Wearing it, he assumed the very spirit of the desert and his stance – legs apart, arms akimbo – added strength to the illusion. But the *kufiyeh* skilfully bound around his arrogantly held head seemed more than anything else to emphasise his return to the customs of the Arab people. Beneath it, his aquiline features had an added sombreness and his dark eyes glistened with primitive fire, newly released so doubly dangerous.

"Yes, thank you, I have had a most enjoyable visit." Her voice was not quite steady, but she discovered that actually she felt able to cope with his projected intimidation. Her earlier encounter had left her armoured, wrapped around in a cloak of security that not even harsh words could penetrate. She withstood his narrow-eyed glance, retreating behind an expression of dreamy unconcern that served to infuriate him.

"I would not have thought the villagers' pleasures sufficiently sophisticated for your taste," he accused her sarcastically.

"What do you know of my tastes?" she countered, incensed. "You do not know me half so well as you imagine, *señor*, nor are you ever likely to!"

He swallowed up the distance between them with one giant stride and smouldered down at her. "Did I imagine the incident aboard ship when you and your accomplice combined to cheat my cousin?" he challenged as if urging her to contradict. "Did my eyes deceive me when I picked up the incriminating cheque made out to yourself by a man you could only have known for mere weeks? And discounting all of that, did I not hear from your own lips the plan you conceived to fool not only my aunt and Isabel but also Alvaro himself! No, *señorita*, I would be a fool ever to allow myself to believe that one so practised in deceit could ever be deserving of mercy!" He swung on his heel, his cloak swirling around him like the wings of a swooping bat and bit out one final savage sentence.

"Sleep well, *señorita*. Tomorrow marks the beginning of a week of ceremonies which custom decrees must precede our much rejoiced-over wedding!"

CHAPTER VI

HAD it not been for Zuela, the activities of the following week would have driven Sara to distraction, wondering if each day's ceremony would be the last before the final act of marriage was performed. Zuela's explanations helped to keep her informed, but even so her nerves were frayed with anxiety and worry to such an extent that she was driven to pleading with Zuela for help to escape.

"Escape?" When Zuela's eyes betrayed a flash of quickly concealed hope Sara's heart leapt with optimism; she had not been wrong about the Arab girl's love for the *señor*; helping to remove a rival for his affections was an action she would hardly be foolish enough to reject. But she had underestimated the hold custom had upon the Arab people. Strongly held beliefs and superstitious fear handed down through generations could not be cast out lightly, not even in a moment of rebellion. Zuela's mouth trembled when she refused. "I'm sorry," she told Sara dully, "but I could not do such a thing to the *señor*."

"But I *hate* him!" Sara shouted in her aggravation. "I will not be forced into marrying a man I dislike, however obscure and meaningless the ceremony!"

"The wishes of the bride are never heeded," Zuela intoned without a flicker of emotion. "Indeed, the consent of the girl is neither required nor asked."

"*Oh!*" Sara's hands clasped and unclasped as she fought to contain the ravages of frustration. For days she had witnessed acts of tradition progressively carried out until now there was less than one day left before the marriage. *One day!* She flinched from reflecting upon the embarrassments she had already suffered and from imagining others that might be in store. How she had hated Felipe for not even attempting to conceal his amusement at the remarks passed by the chiefs of the village whose job it was to assess the value of his future bride. Their faces had registered dismay and not a little scorn as she had stood before them to be looked over by disparaging eyes. Grunting, and pulling mournfully at their beards, they had circled around her, ignoring her scarlet face, intent only upon their search for the signs of strength that were essentially desirable in a Rif bride. Finally, they had thrown up their arms, bewailing loudly some damning facet of her physical appearance. Felipe – and she still burned at the memory – had insisted upon translating their remarks even though he was convulsed with laughter.

"They look for two qualities, *señorita*. The first, youth, is an absolute essential and on that point they have no quarrel, but the second one is plumpness and on that point they say, and I quote: 'If an illness befalls a plump wife, at least something is left of her afterwards; whereas in the case of the one who is already lean ...'" She had stomped away, furious, her ears beseiged by his unkind laughter.

Unconsciously, she made an impatient gesture and glared angrily around the inside of the tent where she and Zuela were relaxing against piles of silken cushions heaped about the floor. Her face softened when she saw Zuela's woebegone expression; she had no right to vent her spleen upon the girl who had been designated to serve her.

"Do cheer up, Zuela," she admonished. "You must learn not to take the things I say in temper so much to heart. I know you would help me if you could, and I understand that your loyalty to the *señor* must come before any duty to myself, so stop moping and smile, for heaven's sake!" Zuela's instant obedience to her command made her feel unbearably dictatorial, so in an effort to dispel some of her own ill humour she changed the subject. "Tell me again what must be endured before the *Dreaded Day*," she capitalized.

Zuela's hand, with fingers outspread, was brought into use as she began counting off previous days' happenings. "First, we had 'the cleaning of the wheat', you remember – four flags were hoisted on top of the *señor's* house and the grain – barley, wheat and durra – that is to be used during the wedding was heaped up in the courtyard to be cleaned by all the unmarried girls of the village?" Sara nodded; she could hardly

121

forget the village chief's barbaric machinations on that occasion. She had watched fascinated while he had sprinkled both the grain and the girls with water as a safeguard against evil spirits. He had then thrust a dagger into one of the heaps, and placed a bowl containing a mixture of raw egg and salt upon its summit; the dagger and salt, Zuela had explained, being directed against evil spirits and the eggs to ensure a happy wedded life. Eventually the bowl and its contents had been buried outside of the tent – which it was supposed would be shared by herself and the *señor* after the ceremony – so that it would be stepped upon by the bridal pair as they entered the tent together for the first time as man and wife.

"You don't need to remind me of number two," Sara interrupted shortly. "That was the night the *señor* and his companions engaged in a disgusting round of revelry that kept us all awake until the early hours."

"But every bridegroom must have a 'bridegroom's night'," Zuela protested. "He would not be considered manly if he did not!"

"Oh, don't bother to recap further," Sara interpolated when Zuela made to continue. "I want to know what happens next, not what has already gone before."

Looking a little unhappy, Zuela obeyed Sara's edict. "Well . . ." she glanced apprehensively at her set face, "tomorrow, you will be thoroughly bathed by the women of the tribe before being painted with henna . . ."

"*What!*" Sara jumped to her feet, bridling like an

aggravated terrier. "You don't seriously believe I would allow . . ."

"But it is necessary," Zuela showed obvious distress. "Such customs must be carefully observed, otherwise Yiblis, the devil, would make husband and wife fight, as he is never pleased about people getting married."

"Then for once I'm on his side," Sara spat. "I can understand why Yiblis, as you call him, should be angered at the thought of losing one of his own!"

"You can't mean the *señor*?" Zuela gasped a protest. "He is the kindest of men, one any woman would be honoured to have as a husband."

"Then I suggest you take my place!" Sara retorted with unthinking cruelty, too blinded by rage to choose her words. But when Zuela's face crumpled she felt ashamed and stricken with remorse. Quickly, she moved to put an arm around the Arab girl's shoulders and whispered an apology. "I'm sorry, Zuela, please try to forget I said that. I'm a stupid, unfeeling woman, and even if you do bring yourself to forgive me I'll never forgive myself."

Zuela's head lifted to show large tear-filled eyes. "You know," she whispered brokenly, "you know, and yet you ask for *my* forgiveness?"

"Yes, I've known for some time that you are in love with the *señor*," Sara smoothed the dark head that was bent with remorse, "but I feel sorrow for you, not anger. He is not worthy of being loved by someone as wonderful as you."

Zuela shook her head fiercely, but did not reply, and Sara's curiosity moved her to ask, "Why do you stay here when his nearness must be torture to you? Why don't you return to your husband's people where Khairy will be able to live the sort of life he is entitled to as the grandson of a Caid?"

Zuela drew a deep breath of pain. "I cannot," she choked. "They will kill him if he ever returns!"

"Kill Khairy?" Shock chilled Sara's blood.

Zuela nodded. "That is why I had to flee from my husband's people as soon as I was able after the birth. You see," she struggled for composure and prepared to explain, "my husband married out of his class, and that in itself is a crime punishable by death in the tribe to which he belongs. Only the intercession of his mother prevented the sentence from being carried out, and when, shortly afterwards, my husband was killed it was looked upon as Kismet – an act of fate. Then, when my child was born deformed, they claimed that he was invaded by *djinns* and that his misfortune was revenge by the gods for the wrong we had committed. Nothing but the execution of my child would appease the gods and exorcise the evil *djinns* contained within his body, they insisted, so I was left no choice but to flee with my child under cover of darkness to escape here to my own people."

Sara rocked back on her heels, wide-eyed with disbelief. "But that's incredible! An impossible situation!" she jerked.

124

"But not such a hopeless one as we once thought," Zuela smiled through her tears. "Señor Felipe has been in touch with my father-in-law, the Caid, who is old and very lonely, and he has promised that if Khairy can be restored to him in perfect physical health he will welcome him as his heir. A doctor friend of the *señor*'s has already examined Khairy and has held out hope that a series of operations will bring about a successful conclusion. So you need hardly wonder," she finished softly, her eyes tender with warmth of feeling, "why I love the *señor*. To me he is the most wonderful of men, the brightest star that shines in my heaven."

Sara flinched; the fervour and sentiment in Zuela's words found an echo in her own heart. For days she had searched the faces of the men of the village, hoping for a clue that might pinpoint the man whose memory had teased her thoughts every moment since their strange encounter. Many times her senses had leapt at the sound of a similar voice or at some vaguely familiar gesture, only to sink back under the blow of yet another disappointment. She could not explain even to herself the attraction he held for her, an attraction so vital that the memory of his touch made her quiver with inward longing and the echo of his words, played back again and again on the sound track of her mind, was a comfort to be hugged close, a treasured talisman that would guard her against Felipe de Panza and his barbaric intentions. She felt his presence so strongly that she was moved into action: today might be the day of their second meeting, but it would hardly be likely to occur within the confines of her tent.

"I'm going outside for some air, Zuela," she decided impetuously. "No, don't bother to come with me," she waved a protest when Zuela would have risen to accompany her. "I'd rather be alone. I need to think, so you might as well remain here as I'll be very morose company." With a smile and a wave, she slipped out of the tent before Zuela's protests could delay her.

Outside, the village had an air of festivity. Everywhere, women were preparing great mounds of food, stirring, dipping, tasting, all to the accompaniment of much chatter and excited laughter. Obviously, tomorrow was to be a great day for them, but Sara shuddered away from dwelling upon the significance it might hold for herself. Her progress through the village was slow as each group of women tried to persuade her to sample the delicacies they were preparing. The aroma of *tajin* – a stew of chicken, pigeon, mutton and beef left to simmer for hours upon a slow heat – was already wafting in the air, together with *harira*, a wonderful thick soup which she had already sampled. Kebabs of mutton, offal and small sausages were being expertly skewered ready to be roasted over glowing charcoal embers in company with whole sheep carcases that were lined up ready to be hoisted on to spits, then turned laboriously hour upon hour until succulently tender.

Her stomach began to knot with apprehension. So sure had she been that some last-minute intervention would baulk Felipe's plans, she had refused to allow herself to worry. But now, as she watched the final preparations going ahead, she had to face, with a sick feeling of dread, the possibility that by this same time tomorrow she could be the wife of the one man in the world she had come to detest.

She stumbled as she hurried away from the groups of laughing women, her mind too numb to register that her feet were leading her into danger. A line of horsemen, young Rif bloods resplendent in gay ceremonial colours, were lined up mounted on brightly caparisoned horses. A pistol shot rang into the air and sent them charging headlong in a frenzied gallop, with heads down and bodies bent low in the saddle to gain maximum speed, too intent upon the race to notice Sara's slight figure wandering blindly in the path of their horses' galloping hooves. A sound like the rumble of approaching thunder was the first indication she received of danger. Her head jerked up and with stricken eyes she saw the line of deadly hooves moving swiftly towards her. Too petrified to move, she stood waiting for death or, if fate were to be unkind, injuries too horrible to be borne. With a flash of almost Eastern fatalism she registered that this could be answer to her problems – Felipe de Panza was, after all, to be cheated of his prey!

The sound of hooves thundered in her ears, a cloud of dust enveloped her completely so that she never actually witnessed her own dramatic rescue when from out of nowhere and with the speed and determination of a man demented, a rider charged across the line of approaching horses to scoop her into his saddle before releasing a volley of rifle shots into the air. All she knew was that during the last terrifying seconds she closed her eyes, then felt herself lifted into the air and thrown across something hard and so unmercifully bumpy that every breath was knocked out of her body. Shots rang out, and she was jerked upright into steel-hard arms just in time to see a sea of horseflesh veer off course and go rushing past in a sweating, steaming wave. Sick and trembling with reaction, she clung to the rider who had snatched her into his arms and buried her face against his cloak while he galloped his horse away from what might have been her place of execution. She sobbed as she clung to the stiff, erect form that sat so tensely in the saddle, then gradually, fear was superseded by relief and by a contentment completely alien to the circumstances when she became aware that the arms holding her were communicating the same possessive, tender quality she had experienced only once before. She nestled against him, her head against his chest, happy to wait until she could savour to the full the wonderful moment when she would look for the first time upon the face of the man whose presence had haunted her dreams, the moment when shadow became substance and she would hear again the magic voice that had the power to disperse every nightmare that plagued her.

The conviction was so strong, she had to bite back

128

a cry of bitter disappointment when the rider drew in the reins and prepared to dismount. His harsh, clipped voice rasped her nerves when he commanded, "If you will loosen your grip on my shirt, *señorita,* I will help you down from the saddle!"

Her eyes were wide and deeply green with shock when they lifted to his face and it took tremendous effort to gather her wits and make the confused reply:

"I'm sorry, *señor,* I might have known it would be you."

"Of course," he answered lightly as he slid to the ground and opened his arms wide to receive her. "Who else has the same interest in keeping you alive? I always protect my property."

"I'm not your property," she clenched, hating the tears that clogged her throat and hating still more the need she felt to offer thanks to the hard-eyed man who had saved her from pain only so that he could inflict his own particular brand of torment at leisure. Without making any attempt to accept the assistance he offered, she remained looking down at him as she whispered: "I wish you had let me die . . .!"

His face darkened. The dusky cloud of hair accentuating her pale cameo face, her vulnerable, drooping mouth and the veiled brilliance of her eyes all spoke of deep unhappiness. He could not doubt that her words were sincerely meant.

"Ah!" His smile held not a vestige of pleasure. "So my methods are achieving success? It is greatly satisfying to learn that you, who have not hesitated to use people to your own ends, are at last being made to suffer. I had wondered from your seeming insensibility if you were a fool, but fools do not suffer pangs of conscience, neither do they react satisfactorily to the more refined methods of punishment." He sounded driven. Although his words were hard, his eyes were tormented, as if some traumatic experience had stripped him for a moment of the hard core of dislike of herself that motivated all his actions.

She swayed in the saddle. Reaction, united with despair, had helped to crush every bit of fight from her aching body. He moved instinctively to catch her when she would have fallen and the small apology she murmured before she fainted into his arms was, ironically and quite unintentionally, the sharpest weapon she had ever used against him.

CHAPTER VII

MUTINOUS and tight-lipped, Sara sat within a circle of excited women all intent upon adorning her with every conceivable aid to beauty. She was far beyond the boundaries of fear; only mere hours ago she had been subjected to the humiliation of being rigorously scrubbed by the village washerwoman whose job it was to wash the bride clean of evil spirits, then half drowned as bucketful after bucketful of water was sluiced over her by the rest of her enthusiastic attendants. Rage was the primary emotion that held her as, like a trussed-up doll, she was dressed in her wedding finery and decorated with stars, crosses and other good luck emblems vital to the success of the ceremony.

Zuela was nowhere to be seen; she had faded out of sight at the arrival of the village women, leaving her to their untender mercies without a word of warning or even an explanation of what was to come. I'll have a few choice words to say to that young woman, Sara seethed inwardly. And to think I supposed her to be my friend! She eyed the giggling, pushing women coldly. She had quickly discovered the uselessness of trying to escape their ministrations. They had been given a job to do and no one was going to be allowed to say it had not been done thoroughly even if, at times, its doing entailed the employment of brute force to subdue the temper of the bride the *señor* had so unwisely chosen. They were too simple to realize she was merely biding her time, Sara comforted herself as she prepared to seize the first opportunity of escaping that presented itself. It would be only too easy to evade them once they had been gulled into thinking her resistance had been subdued. She looked down with distaste upon the costume she had been forced to wear. Trousers made of light, filmy material gathered in at the ankles by jewelled bands, a scanty, bejewelled brassiere top that left little to the imagination, silken slippers and ornate strings of beads – all would better have graced the figure of a harem dancer.

The sound of men shouting sent the women scurrying to the door of the tent where they gathered with their backs towards Sara, forgetting in their curiosity the need for constant vigilance. Quick as a flash, she seized her chance and ran, uncaring of her insubstantial attire, not even stopping to plan her direction. She was through the gate of the stockade with many miles of empty road stretching in front of her before she heard a small commotion in the distance that told her she had been missed. Frantically, she searched the revealing landscape for cover. On the open road she would stand out distinctly and the sloping terraces of the vineyards to her left offered little or no shelter. Her only hope was to lose herself amongst the folds of hills, so she swung sharply right and raced as fast as her flimsy slippers would allow towards the nearest grass-covered shoulder. Her lungs felt ready for bursting when finally she flung herself down in the shade of a solitary tree and lay there panting for breath. She could hear nothing to indicate that she had been followed, so gradually her heartbeats subsided to a steadier pace and she relaxed and began to weigh up her position.

After sombre reflection she had to admit that her sense of victory was premature. She was stuck in the middle of the Rif mountains with neither food nor adequate clothing and without any means of contacting help. She clenched her teeth, determining never to go back to the camp; death from starvation or exposure was preferable to the fate that awaited her there. She stumbled to her feet, obeying an urge to put as many miles as possible between herself and Felipe de Panza and began trudging in the opposite direction. It was a terrible shock when she rounded the next hill to be confronted by an Arab stallion elegantly pawing the ground and tossing its mane while it waited the command of its master, who was sitting a few yards away, his white *djellaba* and turban contrasting starkly against inscrutable features.

"Well, are you ready to discuss terms of surrender?" he questioned dryly, one eyebrow quickening upwards as he studied her dishevelled, very revealing outfit.

She stared back at him. "How did you find me?" she

choked, her eyes swivelling to the silent hills as if accusing them of treachery.

"I've had you in sight from the minute you left camp," he stated with infuriating calmness, "but I decided to allow you time to realize how abortive is your attempt to escape. Are you convinced, or would you prefer to continue for a while? I'll be content to sit here until you are ready to beg for recapture."

"Beg? Never!" she trembled, catastrophically near to tears. "I'd rather wander till I drop than ask for mercy from you!" She took a grip upon her emotions and tilted, "But at least the whole camp now knows what I feel about you! Not even your barbaric brotherhood will be able to accept with an easy conscience a bride as unwilling as I have shown myself to be. You dare not force me to go through with the ceremony now!"

When he threw back his head and laughed she knew her reasoning was faulty. "On the contrary, *señorita*," he twinkled, "your actions have allayed the many misgivings my friends have felt about your suitability as a bride. Quite unknowingly, you conformed to Rif custom by fleeing from your bridegroom on the morning of the wedding – you have shown proof of a modest disposition, and that is a highly regarded trait." He stood up with one easy movement and strode across to look down upon her bent head. She was beaten and he knew it. Far above her, she heard him say almost kindly, "A good general knows when to surrender,

134

señorita. Perhaps you are now ready to admit that you took on too practised an adversary?"

She was so dispirited that for one unguarded moment she was tempted to plead, but then, at the precise moment when her lips parted to speak, she remembered her grandfather's words: *Whatever adversities lie ahead, I know you will meet them with unbowed head and an unbroken spirit!* When her proud head suddenly tilted to show eyes defiant and sparkling green he betrayed a flash of unwilling admiration.

"I'm ready to go back, *señor,*" she ejected through clenched teeth, "but I warn you not to become too complacent. I do not yet admit to being beaten!"

Back at the camp, everyone was gathered in the centre of the compound waiting for the final ceremony to begin. Felipe left her in the charge of the widely grinning attendants and after doing a quick tidying-up of her hair and costume they too disappeared, leaving her alone in the tent with a thumping heart and a mouth so dry she felt she would choke. She longed for Zuela to put in an appearance so that she might answer some of the questions throbbing through her mind, but it was Khairy who appeared at the door of the tent, dressed up to perform some function which, guessing from his puffed-up manner, held some vestige of importance.

"You are ready, *señorita?*" he quavered excitedly, obviously anxious for his part to begin.

"Yes, thank you, Khairy, but before we go won't

you tell me what your duties are to be?"

His chest swelled with pride. "I am to ride in front of your carriage, *señorita*. Always a boy is chosen to ride in front of the bride so that she may be helped to bring forth male offspring!"

Sara's cheeks were still burning when she was helped into the "bridal box" strapped on to a vicious-looking camel. It was a curious structure consisting of wooden framework draped in thick net to shield her from the evil eye. The camel was hung with embroidered rugs and tasselled trappings and musical bells tinkled as it was led slowly towards the crowd of waiting villagers. She did not remember much of the performing of the actual rites. There was a great deal of confusing ritual, a gold coin was pressed to her forehead to ensure prosperity and some brown-coloured paste was pressed first into Felipe's palm and then into her own, but she did not look, much less speak, to the man who was the instigator of the meaningless ceremony. It was only when two little girls came forward to present her with a basket containing henna, sugar plums and slippers that she remembered Zuela remarking that this gift symbolized her entry into the nuptial home and was the culminating act of the ceremony. Only then did she look up at Felipe. She was now his wife or, as more befitted the nature of the marriage, his chattel, his water-carrier, the provisional bearer of his sons . . .

She was not allowed time to analyse whether it was this thought that sent the blood racing madly through her veins or whether it was the lambent flame her quick glance surprised in the depths of his eyes. For long seconds their glances held and it seemed even in the midst of tumultuous rejoicing that they were quite alone while he stamped upon her his own private seal of ownership with a look so compelling and so full of possession that she shuddered from wondering just how much the strange ceremony had meant to the man whose Arab blood so influenced his actions – with such dire consequences to herself!

Feasting and humour were at their highest when a roll of drums was heard above the din being made by the villagers. It heralded the arrival of a small procession of boys who approached the gathering and took up their stand in the centre of the jostling merrymakers. The sound of the drums escalated into a mighty pounding, and a chant was taken up by the villagers when a veiled performer riding a camel was seen approaching. With slow and measured tread the camel, draped with heavy and expensive rugs, wended its way through the crowd. Sara's eyes widened as she recognized, even though veiled, that the rider was Zuela clothed in the dress of a bride.

The camel reached the centre of the space and the boys formed a ring around it; the music swelled to a very high note and every villager joined in, each throat working overtime as they were caught up in a spirit of emotional fervour. Sara watched intently as Zuela balanced herself upon her knees, then began to wave her arms and bend and sway her body in time to the music. Her movements became gradually more fluid, the chanting villagers egging her on to fantastic bodily expressions of emotion such as might be felt by a girl swept by the spirit of unwedded youth. Then presently the chanting villagers egging her on to fantastic bodily fied and more attuned to the symbolizing of married life with all its pain and joy. It was so beautifully and so sensitively portrayed that Sara felt an emotion so deep it was a lump in her throat. So much so that when finally a much slower note was introduced and the dance terminated in a portrayal of the oncoming of women's old age tears stung behind her eyelids and she had to swallow hard to overcome the effect the exquisitely performed dance had upon her senses.

Felipe's words were an intrusion when, after appraising her expressive face, he commented, "So, you are beginning to recognize that Rif customs do not benefit only the men of the tribe. Zuela has portrayed the ecstasy and the pain, the glory and the subjugation that are the inheritance of every bride whether cultivated or savage. The Rif are primitive in their passions, but every woman taken by them as a wife is counted fortunate in acquiring a faithful and devoted mate."

Sara looked up, full of sudden defiance. "In return for what?" she asked. "Demonstrating a perfect obedience? Prostrating herself submissively before her husband in such a way as to have no will of her own? If that is Rif justice then you can keep it, *señor*. I prefer the more emancipated outlook of Western civilization! "

They were surrounded by feasting villagers, sitting next to the head men of the tribe, so it was impossible to argue without betraying animosity. He bent towards her, his teeth showing white as he flashed a smile, but his eyes so full of cold intent she shivered. "Rif justice, primitive though it might be, is more merciful than any you dispense. I have no doubt many of your past acquaintances would rejoice if they knew that at last you are on the receiving end of the same callous indifference you have meted out to them in the past! "

She glared back, feeling an urge to smack his despicably regal face, but a reminder of the reprisals he had threatened should that act ever be repeated stayed her hand. Instead, she had to be content with blasting scorn from her stormy eyes. Her belligerence was so marked that attention was riveted upon them both, so, blandly, and to her utter confusion, he lifted the most choice morsel from his plate and held it to her lips as an invitation to eat. There was complete silence from the assembled company as they waited for her reaction. *"Don't dare!"* he breathed, as her mouth pursed in a suggestion of refusal. His eyes never left her lips as they wavered, unsure of the threat behind his words, then finally parted to accept the proffered bite. Relief rippled through the watching men before they relaxed once more into enjoyment of their pleasures. The woman was untamed; they themselves would never countenance such a wife, but the *señor* seemed satisfied so all must be well. His needs were different from theirs, his standards strange, but in the words of one of their elders: "There must be much in the woman that only his eyes can see – after all, the hawk is not content to catch flies . . ."

It was both a relief and a strain when after darkness fell, she was escorted by women holding lighted torches to the doorway of the tent. She was left there alone and shivering while they circled the tent three times muttering incantations she was now able to recognize as efforts to ward off evil spirits. Her flimsy bridal apparel gave no protection against the wind that had sprung up with the sun's departure, and she gritted her teeth to stop them from chattering as cold, both physical and spiritual, chilled her body. She smothered a gasp when, encouraged by a mighty cheer, Felipe descended from out of the darkness to scoop her up in his arms and carry her into the tent. She clung to the folds of his cloak, forgetting in her distress to fear the body whose warmth she coveted. Even when he set her down she could not bear to withdraw from the comfort he emanated, and she signalled mute gratitude when he shrugged out of his cloak and slid it around her icy slimness.

"I'm sorry my forgetfulness has caused you physical distress," he clamped as his hands rubbed briskly over the heavy cloak to generate welcome heat. Her teeth chattered, so when she tried to reply he pulled her forward, cloak and all, into his arms, employing his vibrant body as a furnace to combat her frozen misery. For long minutes she basked in the comfort of his warmth, her head against the powerful heart that was radiating heat from his body to hers. She had become chilled to the bone during the short time she was exposed to the wind, and the sudden transition from cold to heat caused her to feel drowsy and to enter the same state of euphoria often experienced by a cosseted and terribly weary child.

"M . . . m . . . m," she sighed, and nestled closer, her heavy eyelids drooping over eyes bemused with the desire for sleep. He lifted her incredibly gently and strode across to the pile of cushions that made up her bed. Still wrapped around by his cloak, she was laid down, but when he straightened to leave her her fingers refused to be prised from the grip they had upon his shirt. Even in sleep, her hold was intense, so he had no choice but to sit cradling her like a slumbering child while he waited until she should awake.

The camp was still and silent when hours later her eyelids lifted over sleep-drugged eyes. She felt warm and cherished, cradled by reassuring arms. Still in the no-man's-land between sleep and full alertness, she sighed and snuggled closer, then smiled with complete contentment when the arms around her tightened protectively.

"Are you awake?" The whispered question set her quivering, but she remained silent, hardly daring to hope in case she might again repeat the mistake she

141

had made once before. His sigh when she did not answer almost made her abandon pretence, but she was pleased she had not when his hand reached out to stroke her hair and she heard him whisper the words that convinced her she had at last found the shadowy presence who stalked her mind.

"Brave little warrior!" Only he had ever called her that! In a fever of impatience, hungry for the sight of the man whose memory tormented her, she turned to face him, only to fall back, incredulous, when she saw Felipe de Panza.

"Why did you use those words? How could you possibly know . . . ?" The cry was wrung from her, disillusionment, pain, bitter disappointment, they were all contained in the agonized questions. The interior of the tent was dim, the lamps turned low so that the mellow pool of light surrounding them was hazed by confusing shadows cast by flickering wicks. But there was no doubting the identity of the man who stared back at her, betraying for one fleeting second a flash of acute desire. It was so quickly disguised she could almost have believed she had imagined it, were it not that his incriminating words still rang in her ears.

"It was you!" She sobbed out the accusation, her heart thudding hard against her ribs. "I suppose that, too, was part of my punishment. You were playing up to me and I thought . . ."

"You thought what?" His voice was barely recognizable when he breathed out the words. "When you

believed me to be a stranger you felt an attraction —
perhaps even love?"

"Love *you*?" Her look radiated contempt. "You are
a despot, a spoiler of people's lives, so how can you
ever expect to know love?"

He jerked her forward to stare down at her with
eyes mirroring cold passion. "If I know nothing of
love then teach me!" he rasped, pulling her closer. Fear
rose up inside her as she sensed danger. She was alone,
completely unprotected from the desires of a man
filled with dangerous madness!

Her puny defences were stormed with an ease that
was frightening. Pinned against his hard strength, she
was subjected to kisses of sweet steel that threatened
to tear the heart from her body. Against her pulsating
throat she heard his demented whisper, "You are a fever, a disease in my blood that's past cure or reason. I
know you to be a cheat and a liar, Sara Battle, but at
this moment in time I could not care less . . .!" And the
numbing, terrifying truth was that as his lips clung to
hers and his touch awakened within her a wild and joy-
ous unrest she discovered that she did not care either.

The peak of emotion was almost reached when she
was thrust suddenly at arm's length. He held her away,
fighting visibly for control, then just as suddenly withdrew from her completely. Quivering uncontrollably,
she watched through a mist of tears as he strode without a backward glance through the doorway of the tent,
then with a moan of despair she sank down upon the

cushions and began, even though convulsed with sobs, to search her mind for excuses that might allow her to forgive her own weakness in responding so fervently to the man she had pledged herself to hate.

CHAPTER VIII

THEY left the village early next morning to return to Tangier. Sara learned of Felipe's decision from Zuela who came to the tent to serve breakfast, a duty she performed in complete silence while managing, nevertheless, to project the sympathy she felt at the sight of Sara's wan face and tear-shadowed eyes. But she made no comment on the absence of the *señor*, whose breakfast she had also provided, but merely removed the superfluous dishes from the tray and deposited them outside before returning to sit quietly until Sara was ready to speak.

"I'm sorry, Zuela, I can't eat any more." She pushed away her plate with the food barely touched.

Zuela inclined her head, understanding perfectly, but anxiety moved her to protest, "You have far to go, *señora*, please try to eat just a little more."

With a dispirited hand Sara pushed back a heavy wave of hair that had fallen across her brow and struggled for a second to clarify Zuela's words. "Far to go?" she echoed stupidly.

"But yes," Zuela's dark eyes were sad. "Even now the *señor* is preparing to leave us, and he is hardly likely to leave behind his wife of so few hours. Tangier was mentioned, but his mood is such that no one dares to question him further. He seems very ... displeased, *señora*, but perhaps you could charm him into staying?" she appealed.

Sara's laugh held an element of hysteria and Zuela forbore to press the point. Something was very wrong, of that there was no doubt, and her heart ached for the girl whose expressive face reflected deep unhappiness.

"Is there anything I can do to help, *señora*?" she dared to ask, only to be disconcerted by the sharp reply.

"Yes, you can stop calling me *señora*. Also you can leave me alone, *for heaven's sake leave me alone!*"

Sara felt absolutely wretched as she watched Zuela's dignified departure, but she could not bear the company of anyone; even Zuela's gentle presence rasped like a file against her sensitive nerves. The news that they were leaving for Tangier should have brought her relief, but her mind was unable to grapple with any fact other than the one that had kept her awake, unbelieving and not a little distrait, all during the night. She was in love with Felipe! Not even by speaking the words aloud could she dispel the fantasy they contained. The hard conclusion had been reached during long hours of searching both her conscience and her heart until she had at last forced herself to face the truth she had been deliberately evading. It had not been mere coincidence that had ordained that her mysterious companion of the shadows should have the height and build of Felipe, nor that he should emanate the same sense of assurance. Deep down, without even admitting their existence, she had admired these qualities in the man who was her enemy, qualities personal to Felipe alone which she in her blind stubbornness had attempted to bestow upon a shadow rather than admit to them in the substance. For reasons of his own he had played up to her that night; he had listened, sympathized, even comforted, and on that solitary occasion, under the guise of strangers, their first meeting had been like a tryst made many years ago . . .

Khairy burst into the tent, scattering her thoughts and demanding her complete attention. "*Señora, señora,* my mother says you have to leave! I do not want you to leave, *señora,* I love you, my mother loves you. Please, please stay!" His black eyes were moist and his lip trembled as he searched her face for reassurance. His distress was echoed in her voice when she told him gently,

"I love you too, Khairy, and I count your mother one of my dearest friends, but I have no choice. If the *señor* has decided to leave then I must go with him."

"Spoken like a true Rif bride!" a hard voice mocked from the doorway. They both spun round to face Felipe, once more a son of Spain, his suit immaculately pressed and his dark head free of the Riffish turban that had more than any other thing emphasised his affinity to the Arab race.

Khairy ran towards him, ready to plead, but for once

the *señor* had no time to spare for him. His hard look was fastened upon Sara, taking in the cloudy mass of hair that tumbled around her peaked face, its colour contrasting sharply against skin that had the pallor of marble. Her mouth was unsteady with pain, and the green eyes from which all sparkle had fled seemed to aggravate him greatly, as was borne out by the curtness of the command that scythed across the width of the tent to deal her a pitiless blow.

"We are returning to Tangier immediately. I have no doubt the news will lend wings to your feet and that you will not keep me waiting longer than is absolutely necessary, but that will suit me admirably. My mission is accomplished and the sooner we leave the better!"

Mission accomplished! All during the return journey his words echoed in her mind. She was being taken back to Tangier to be held before Alvaro as a hostage to prevent him from ever again rebelling against marriage to Isabel. She was a marked woman; she could not have been more possessed if she had been branded, and Alvaro would never again dare to cast eyes in her direction. But the irony of it all! To think that if Felipe could have brought himself to believe her capable of telling the truth all this need never have happened . . .

He swung the jeep off the road and brought it to an abrupt halt. They had been travelling for some hours without once stopping and obviously he was feeling the need of refreshment. He unloaded fruit and a bottle of wine from the back of the jeep and strode to the edge of a nearby stream where he spread out a blanket upon which he deposited the alfresco meal before returning to her. She was sitting still as a mouse, her hands folded in her lap, staring into the distance as if waiting for some symbol of hope to appear on the horizon.

"Come," he held out a hand to help her down, "there are things we must discuss before we reach the villa, and now is as good a time as any." Without argument, she climbed down from the jeep, so pointedly ignoring his proffered hand that a hint of angry colour ran under his skin. They ate in silence until the fruit was finished, then, when she refused wine, he poured out a measure for himself and studied her intently while he drank. When he did speak his words were so startling that she jumped.

"You are a very beautiful woman, Sara. It is not surprising you are likened to Cleopatra whose beauty proved so fatal."

Her face suffused by hot colour, she stammered, "Is ... is there nothing you do not know about me, señor? Do you make it your business to collect every bit of gossip that comes your way?"

Lazily he rolled on his side and admitted, "From our first meeting I found you interesting. Women of your qualities are mercifully rare, especially within one's family circle. I cannot say I altogether blame you for wanting the respectability of Alvaro's name, and I hope that you, in turn, will understand my motives in preventing such an occurrence. However," he gave careful attention to the lighting of a cheroot, "now that the battle is won, I must confess I feel I owe you something. Why I should feel this way I cannot imagine, unless it is simply that the mock ceremony was not such a mockery after all and the rites, barbaric though they were, have impressed upon my conscience an obligation towards you that only a proper marriage will assuage." He swivelled towards her, cold mockery playing upon his lips at the sight of her obvious perplexity, and stressed, "I'm offering to marry you, *señorita*, legally and in the sight of my family and friends! Well, what have you to say? As Señora de Panza you will be even richer and more secure than you would be as Señora de Leon."

Her cheeks burned at the coolly offered insult. Her immediate impulse was to reject his proposal with words so searing that they would leave him in no doubt of the distaste she felt for his suggestion. But she pulled up sharply as she noticed the restless pulling on his cheroot that betrayed a tautness completely at odds with his relaxed body. Were his words perhaps not so illogical as they sounded? Her mind went back to the moment after the marriage ceremony when his look had burned possession upon her very soul. However lightly he had entered into the idea of a mock marriage, in that instant he had been profoundly moved. And later that evening when they were alone together, only tremendous will power had prevented him from taking what he so strongly desired — *what he felt was his by right to take!*

She felt no triumph at the discovery of his weakness. He wanted her so badly he was willing to hide his desire under a cloak of obligation, so deceiving himself that the outcome he sought had actually been thrust upon him. She had waited so long for the tide to turn in her favour, but now that the moment had arrived she hesitated to act upon it. When passion had been at its highest he had admitted she was a drug in his veins. Dared she take the chance of becoming his wife, allowing him to think her motives mercenary? Or had she the strength to refuse him, knowing that once back in Tangier she might never see him again?

"Well, what have you decided?" His tone was casual to the point of indifference.

She swallowed hard, then asked carefully, "Are you asking me to believe that you want to marry a person you despise — someone you believe to be a cheat, a gambler, a preyer upon men — simply to ease a fretful conscience?"

His dark eyes were slumbrous as they roved her fresh young beauty. As if compelled by an inner urge, he admitted, "Perhaps I am hoping that a marriage between us might produce some hidden compensations." Then his voice took on a quality of roughness as, impatient of prevarication, he demanded, "Are you or are you not to be Señora de Panza?"

For the life of her she could not hold back the breathless whisper: "To be!"

Her answer seemed to afford him little satisfaction. A blush spread all over her body as she was scrutinizing by eyes of pinpointed steel that roved her face seeking answers to unspoken questions. Her shame was such that she would have retracted, but then he sprang suddenly to his feet and stated so matter-of-factly: "Good, then we had better be on our way," that she was able to swallow her misgivings and follow him to the jeep to continue the journey.

Halfway to Tangier, he made a surprise detour, deserting the main road in favour of a secondary one that climbed upwards until they reached a pass affording a breathtaking panorama of softly rounded mountains, then shortly afterwards he took a left fork and as they continued along the steep road she saw in the distance tall minarets towering above the rooftops of a small town. He drove into the centre of a small circular "square" and pulled up outside a *parador* whose sign "Hotel de Chaouen" indicated the name of their stopping place.

"I thought you might welcome a chance to freshen up before arriving at the villa," he offered as explanation. "If you wait here I'll find out if they can oblige us with the use of a room and shower as well as providing us with lunch." He strode into the hotel, leaving her happily assessing what she could see of the delightful old town. It was magnificently positioned high on the mountain tops, with innumerable streams running down to irrigate the flower-filled gardens so beloved by Moroccans. She sniffed deeply, inhaling perfume drifting from the flowering trees planted around the market place, and lifted her face to feel the caress of the breeze being breathed over the town from the surrounding mountains.

"We are in luck," he informed her as he returned to assist her from the jeep. "If you go inside someone will show you to your room while I make arrangements to have our luggage taken upstairs." With a spontaneous grin he added, "I am thankful that you are not like my aunt and Isabel in one respect at least. They have never been known to travel more than a few miles without a pile of luggage, whereas you seem to manage perfectly with one small suitcase." She flushed and shyly returned his smile before leaving him to enter the hotel where she was shown into a room, unobtrusively comfortable, its standards conforming to the Government-run *paradors* in Spain – reasonably priced halting places built in styles typical of their region. She flung off her jacket and stretched luxuriously; somehow her spirits had miraculously revived, and it had all to do with that unexpected grin of Felipe's. Strange how a smile can cure the wounding of a frown. How wonderful it would be to bask for ever in the warmth of his approval . . .

He knocked on her door just as she was giving a final brush to her hair. Her feet seemed hardly to touch the

153

ground as she sped to open it, eager to discover whether
the upward quirk of his lips would tell her his humour
was still mellow. He drew in a quick breath. She was
aware that the pale yellow dress she had chosen to
wear complemented her jet-black hair to perfection,
and that its simple lines drew tantalizing attention to
the slenderness of her figure, but she did not know
that happiness had lent to her movements the vibrant
gracefulness of a young gazelle and had transformed
the jewelled brilliance of her eyes to the softer, gentler
glow reminiscent of an ocean's depths. For one startled
moment his look betrayed flame, flame which was instantly suppressed but which lingered slumbrously as a
lambent glow.

She felt a quiver of pleasure when his deeply timbred
voice complimented: "You look enchanting. Nothing
lunch has to offer will be half so delectable as the
companion I am to share it with." He proffered an arm.
"Are you quite ready?" Without daring to trust her
voice, she took it in silence and allowed him to escort her
downstairs.

They ate spicy soup served piping hot, followed by
pastilla – pigeon and almond pie enclosed in flaky
pastry made with butter — followed by various types of
sweetmeats. It was only when they had been served with
the mint tea that is the drink which inevitably accom-
panies every Moroccan meal that he leant back, well
satisfied, to surprise her once again by offering casually,
"As we are no longer in any hurry to reach Tangier, I

suggest we pay a visit to the *souks*. Chaouen is famous for its excellent local craftmanship, so I'm sure you will find it entertaining. Would you like that?"

The prospect of seeing at first hand one of the wonders of the East made her forget her nervousness and she reacted with a pleased anticipation that brought an indulgent smile to his lips. "Will there be snake-charmers, and jugglers and acrobats?" Her breathless question betrayed the hushed wonder of a child to whom such treats are rare. The once-a-year visits to the circus provided by the orphanage had been something of an aggravation, a whetting of the appetite for such novel entertainment that lingered still in the mind of the girl who should have long outgrown such childish pleasures. His smile betrayed his thoughts and embarrassed colour flared in her cheeks as she fought an onrush of foolishness. As expected, he laughed, but then he confused her by promising gravely,

"If there are no acrobats then I shall demand that they be sent for. You have been sufficiently deprived, and today we must try to make up for the magic stolen from your childhood." His lean fingers reached out to capture her hand that was plucking at a discarded napkin as he reminded her that it was he who had been the recipient of her frightened confidences on the night she had encountered him as a shadowy stranger. She looked away, confused by the complexity of the man whose charm was such he could quell the fury of a stallion as easily as he could charm a band of unruly

youngsters. She wanted to distrust him, to have time
to sort out in her mind the reasons behind his devastating change of attitude, but her worst enemy was her
own desire to be loved that was forcing from her mind
every niggling doubt about his motives. *Live for today*,
her grandfather had urged. Well, just this once, she
would take his advice!

To set foot in the labyrinth of alleyways comprising
the main *souk* was to step immediately into the Middle
Ages. From the very beginning of their tour Sara was
engrossed in the fascinating stalls and shops that held
for her a magic so intense she could not find adequate
words to express her pleasure. But her green eyes, wide
with wonder, reflected her feelings perfectly, so dispensing with any need for speech.

Felipe was an expert and considerate guide. He ela-
borated in depth as he explained the methods and materials used by the craftsmen who were manufacturing
and plying their wares in exactly the same way that their
ancestors had done hundreds of years before. He waited patiently while she hesitated before a potter at his
wheel, watching his nimble fingers shaping a mound of
wet clay into an elegant vase in a matter of seconds.
All around him were stacked finished products, glazed
and painted with colourful patterns of flowers or geo-
metrical designs – no two alike. They then wandered
passed spice perfumed grocers' shops; stalls piled high
with decorated leatherwork, and others offering beaten

metal trays, daggers with inlaid hilts and glittering, barbaric jewellery.

"You must have a memento of your first visit to the *souks*," Felipe's amused voice reached through her absorption as she rummaged through a pile of costume jewellery that had caught her attention. With an embarrassed flush, she hastily dropped the bracelet she was holding and replied,

"No, really, there's no need, just to look is enough." Narrowed eyes denoted his surprise at her reaction and she blushed deeper, hating the thought of being judged mercenary. Ignoring her protest, he sharply directed the grinning Arab to keep the rubbish he displayed for gullible tourists and to bring forward wares more worthy of the lady whose custom would make him the most honoured shopkeeper in the *souk*. Bowing, and with much gesticulation, he hastened to obey, and seconds later he reappeared carrying trays containing trinkets of such delicate beauty that Sara was enraptured.

"Do you have a preference?" he asked, his disparaging hand sorting through the glittering, gem-encrusted baubles.

"They're all so lovely," she breathed, then added a hasty protest, "and so expensive . . ."

"Nonsense!" he laughed. "Although this rogue would have us believe otherwise," he nodded towards the Arab who returned the nod vigorously, "these stones are far from perfect and so sell relatively cheaply." His dark glance disconcerted her as it swung to her face. "Did you really think I would consider such trinkets worthy of anything other than whimsical keepsakes? As my future wife," he watched with interest the slow tide of colour that rose under her clear skin, "you will wear only perfect stones brought to life by masterly cutting — a delicate science that uncovers hidden beauty." He flicked her wavering lashes with the tip of his finger as he continued. "Emeralds are a must, for eyes such as yours can only be matched by that costly and most coveted of stones – the fire emerald."

"You know a lot about precious stones?" she faltered, her taste in jewellery suddenly seeming terribly unsophisticated.

Smiling slightly, he admitted, "I have studied the subject, but only as a hobby. Colourful, sparkling stones have a strong appeal to the imagination, and I find it interesting that even in the days of Moses the Hebrews related the different coloured stones to various phases of life and nature ... What month were you born?" he disconcerted her by suddenly asking.

"April," she stammered. "April the seventh."

His lips quirked at some hidden joke. "Then your natal stone is the diamond, whose white colour symbolizes life, joy and innocence." She turned away to hide a glint of tears as the source of his amusement became clearly apparent. His words were sword-points of mockery, inflicted deliberately to cause pain. She must never again allow herself to be gulled into thinking his attitude towards her had softened; deep within him lurked an outraged conscience shrieking out against his acceptance of a girl whose character fell far short of the standard he himself had attained.

When he turned his attention once more to the choosing of a trinket she was composed enough to accept with a show of gratitude the slender pearl and diamond bracelet he finally selected. But when he clasped it around her wrist his fingers lingered, his caressing, easy strokes upon her smooth skin seeming to denote a pride in possession she found abhorrent. She did not want to be possessed for physical reasons; her heart cried out for understanding and for a love that would withstand the test of time and adversity. Instead of that, all she was offered was pride of ownership and a desire strong enough to overcome the better judgement of a man noted for his iron will.

It seemed no time at all before the sun began to set over the dusty, heat-scorched market place and the majority of stallholders began to pack up their wares. Sara swallowed her disappointment and resigned herself to returning to the hotel without having savoured the amusements she had so eagerly looked forward to – and which Felipe had all but promised. But he made no move to leave. He continued sauntering around, saying little, but with a humorous quirk to his lips that was annoying in its secrecy. Then suddenly, as if by magic, the whole square was filled with performers of every sort – musicians, jugglers, acrobats, swallowers of swords and boiling water, snake-charmers, dancers and, most remarkable of all, storytellers who gathered around them an audience of spellbound listeners who seemed impervious to the discordant noises assailing them from every side.

Felipe's smile widened into a broad grin as he enjoyed her dawning bewilderment. Speech was impossible, the racket being made by performers, collectors, audiences, water-sellers, cab-drivers and would-be guides was deafening. She watched with amazement as a young cyclist pedalled up to the crowd encircling a storyteller, dropped his bike and himself to the ground and became immediately absorbed in the storyteller who never for one moment allowed his grip upon his listeners to relax. "In a few minutes," Felipe spoke close in her ear, "he will reach a climax in his story and stop to pass around the hat." Sure enough he did, and the spell he had cast upon his audience was so great that they could not rid themselves quickly enough of the small coins needed to ensure that the tale would continue.

Felipe dispensed money liberally as they visited each performer; they joined hands and laughed together like children at the antics of the clowns and jugglers, watched spellbound the incredible feats performed by acrobats, and were impressed by the fluidity and grace of the dancers. Some enterprising businessman had built a rooftop café from which vantage point could be seen most of the spectator rings, and it was towards this that he was guiding her when she suddenly stopped, transfixed with horror, staring at a cardboard box lying directly in her path. She tried to scream a warning, but her throat was dry with fear as she watched a cobra's head lift fractionally above the box and begin swaying, its beady eyes fixed directly upon herself, its forked tongue darting horribly in and out as it waited for a victim. Just at that second Felipe saw it too, and with a speed that left her gasping he pushed her out of the way, seized a larger box from a pile of rubbish and thrust it over the writhing snake, effectively blocking its exit. The crowd around the nearby snake-charmer was scythed apart as Felipe strode his way through to grab the luckless man by the scruff of the neck. Biting anger was evident in his every word and gesture as he slated the man for his carelessness, shaking him every now and again to emphasise his displeasure. Finally he dropped the abject Arab in disgust and strode back to Sara, whose ashen face and uncontrollable trembling turned his anger to quick compassion. His arms were a haven, his voice caressingly tender as he rocked her in his arms and soothed gently,

"Forget it, *cara*, the danger is past, you no longer need to fear."

With deliberate effort she pulled herself together. "I'm sorry, but it was so horrible. I was terrified, I thought . . ."

"Hush," he erased the quiver from her mouth with a tender finger. They were quite alone, surrounded by noise but isolated in the depth of shadows between two deserted stalls. The clamour of the market place faded to a whisper as her eyes were drawn to linger, as if hypnotized, by the flame in the depths of his eyes. With a quick intake of breath he pulled her closer, and her heart jerked alive when she felt his lips feathering lightly across her brow. His voice was barely audible when he murmured inconsequentially, "It would not have struck, you know. Snakes like heat and the slightest drop in temperature makes them sluggish." Punctuating his words with teasing kisses, he mused on, "The disgruntled Arab probably threw the snake into its box because it refused to perform and then forgot to put on the lid. He deserved a verbal thrashing, don't you think . . .?"

She nodded, too bemused even to think, then began to tremble when his lips descended, firm and cool, to begin the first exploratory kiss of tenderness they had ever shared. Its sweetness made her senses soar, excitement raced through her veins so that she was able to forget for a few short seconds that his kiss was a kiss of ownership, his action a right to which any future husband might think himself entitled.

"Cleopatra," he sighed against her lips, "you are well named, *bella!*" She stiffened and pulled sharply away, only to suffer being pulled back into steel-hard arms that threatened to break her in two with force of passion. Sharply, his eyes scoured her face, seeking a reason for her withdrawal, but when she turned away and refused to meet his challenge his arms dropped to his sides and he accused bleakly, "So, though my wealth may be greater than Alvaro's my charm is not, eh?" When she did not reply, his voice grated out the instruction, "We must set off for Tangier immediately if we are to arrive before the household retires for the night. Tomorrow will be a big day for us. As soon as our betrothal is announced I shall move heaven and earth to expedite the date of our wedding." She flinched as if from a threat, but managed to hold back the scorching tears burning her throat. The day had been a delight, full of precious moments, but the sun had gone in and once more she felt the chill of his disapproval.

Just one room was illuminated when they pulled up outside the villa shortly before midnight. The night had turned cold and she was glad to obey when he curtly told her to go inside to see about food and hot drinks while he put away the jeep. She heard voices coming from the small salon and decided to announce their arrival first before proceeding to the kitchen in search of the servants. No flash of premonition prepared her for the surprise she received when with a smile of anticipation she flung open the door to confront Isabel and Alvaro who were talking to a stranger whose back was towards her. When Isabel cried out at the sight of her, the stranger turned swiftly and with a gasp of relief held out his arms.

"Sara! I've been worried sick, why on earth didn't you answer my letters?"

"Marc!" Half laughing, half crying, she ran into his arms to be hugged close with a fervour that communicated without words the anxiety and heartburning her silence had caused him. "I meant to write, Marc, honestly I did, but things happened so swiftly," she babbled happily between hugs that were forcing the breath from her body. "I'm sorry if you've been worried . . . How is your father? Are you back in Tangier for good . . .?" His kiss effectively silenced the many other questions she wanted to ask, and she surrendered to its warmth like a kitten to the fire, basking in the deep affection of the man whose regard she had missed more than she had realized.

"It is obvious, Sara, that you and this gentleman are old . . . *friends*." Felipe's clipped words and the emphasis he placed upon his last word robbed their greeting of its aura of friendship, leaving them feeling their relationship had been somehow tainted, smeared by a smutty finger. She knew Marc felt it too, when his arms dropped to his sides and he stepped in front of her to shield her from threatened unpleasantness.

"I don't believe I have had the pleasure?" She could hardly believe it was Marc who was speaking in a tone so frigid one could almost hear the ice splintering around his words. Felipe stood in the doorway, his eyes narrowed to slits, his manner arrogantly demanding an explanation. The antagonism between them both could be felt as they weighed each other up, their tempers so finely balanced the others were afraid to speak in case

164

a careless word should detonate an explosion that might annihilate them all.

Felipe's set expression did not alter when he contradicted coldly, "Your lapse of memory is excusable, Monsieur Rochefort, our first meeting was brief and you had a plane to catch."

A flicker of puzzlement relaxed Marc's tense young face, then memory dawned. "But of course, you are the gentleman who rescued the cheque!"

"That is a matter I intend to discuss with you, *monsieur*," Felipe put in brusquely, leaving Sara frantically wondering what he intended saying to Marc. "At a time and place convenient to us both we must talk, but Sara and I have had a tiring journey, so if you will please excuse us . . . ?"

The dismissal was so insultingly clear that Marc's colour rose, but to his credit he swallowed back an angry retort and began taking his leave with meticulous politeness, lingering only long enough to plead with Sara as he bent over her hand, "I must speak with you alone. May I see you tomorrow? Perhaps we could lunch together?"

Flags of colour were high in her cheeks when she defied the hard eyes that bored into her back and accepted gently, "Of course, Marc, I would enjoy lunching with you. Don't bother to call for me, I'll meet you outside the hotel at one o'clock, if that's all right with you?"

Marc shot a look of triumph at Felipe before bend-ing his head to kiss the hand she held out to him.

"Perfect, *chérie*, I shall count the hours! I am staying at the *pension* if by chance you should want to get in touch with me. *Au revoir, ma petite*, until tomorrow!"

"I'm sorry to disappoint you, *monsieur*, but that will not be possible!" Marc's head jerked up when Felipe coldly addressed him. Blue eyes clashed with black across Sara's head, but Felipe forestalled Marc's angry protest by rebuking her with deceiving mildness, "Have you forgotten, *cara*, that tomorrow we will be kept busy with arrangements for our wedding? You must also have a ring," his laughter was dangerously light when he questioned an astonished Marc, "Would you believe any girl could forget such an important matter? I fear your surprise presence has driven all thought of our wedding from my fiancée's head!"

Isabel's squeal of delight drew attention away from Marc, who stood as if turned to stone, grey-faced with shocked disbelief. "You have fixed a date? Oh, what wonderful news!" As she ran to embrace Sara excited questions tumbled from her lips. "When is the wedding to be? Will it take place here, or in Spain? Can I be bridesmaid, Sara? I would so love to be a bridesmaid just once before I become a bride!"

Sara could not answer; she was staring mutely at Marc, willing him to understand that she would have given anything to have spared him the shock he had so obviously suffered. At that moment she hated Felipe for the deliberately callous way he had sent out to inflict the maximum of shock upon the man he obviously considered as a rival. His dog-in-the-manger attitude was unforgivable; the possession of herself had assumed paramount importance since his sensing of the interest of another man. Heaven help her, she thought bitterly, if she should ever digress when she was his wife. Already, in the light of a mere betrothal, she felt stamped with the hallmark of his domination.

Marc made a tremendous recovery. He still looked stunned, but he managed a smile as he took Sara's hand to ask, "Is this what you want, *petite*?" He jerked his head in Felipe's direction, not yet ready to meet his sardonic look. "Is he really the one who warms your heart?" The torment reflected in his eyes was almost her undoing. She was tempted to ease his hurt with a denial, but that would have meant raising his hopes yet again and she had suffered herself the agony and ecstasy of wishful thinking. So she spared him by being brutal. "Yes, Marc, Felipe is the one I am going to marry."

His head lifted, and with the expressionless face of a man who refuses to acknowledge pain, he addressed Felipe. "Congratulations, *señor*, you are in my opinion the luckiest man in the world. But be warned," his short laugh deceived no one, "if you should ever become careless of your good fortune there are those who will not hesitate to take it into their keeping."

Felipe's lips tightened, but he ignored the veiled threat and curtly repeated his earlier dismissal. "Thank you, *monsieur*. But now, although I insist upon a future meeting, I must ask you again to excuse us as both Sara and I have had a long and tiresome journey . . ." Before he left Marc clicked his heels and bowed to each in turn, but as she watched his retreating figure Sara felt a sense of shame, a feeling that a cherished friendship had been somehow betrayed . . .

Alvaro caught her by the arm when she would have rushed blindly past him to seek the solitude of her room. Isabel, after a perceptive look at her drawn face, had gone to order refreshments and Felipe was escorting Marc to the door to ensure, Sara had no doubt, that his unwelcome guest was speeded on his way. So they were quite alone when Alvaro voiced his incredulous question.

"Sara, what does all this mean? You're surely not seriously considering marriage to Felipe?" She flinched from his intense grip; carried away by amazement, he was completely unaware of the pain he was inflicting. Her green eyes took on a depth he could not fathom when she stumbled over words of explanation.

"Yes, Alvaro, I'm afraid I am. We . . . I . . . it's difficult to say exactly how it happened, I'm not quite sure myself, but . . ."

"He's forcing you to marry him, isn't he?" Alvaro interrupted savagely. "He'd go even as far as that to get you away from me! But why are you allowing it, Sara, *why*? You hate him, you told me yourself you would never forgive the wrong he did your grandfather, and yet now you are asking me to believe you are willing to marry him. I utterly refuse to believe it! If you won't admit the real reason behind your decision then I shall go to Felipe and tell him everything. He has never attempted to hide his contempt of you and he must be made to drastically revise his opinion even if it means making him aware of the true facts!"

"No, Alvaro," an agitated quiver disturbed her mouth, "you promised me you would keep silent and you must keep your word."

He searched her pleading face with dismayed intensity. "But you *can't* marry him knowing he thinks ill of you, and knowing also that, being the man he is, he will never allow himself to love where he cannot respect. He must be told the truth, Sara, *he must!*"

"No! No!" She was trembling with reaction as she gasped out, "How can I tell him I set out deliberately to trick him? That I planned and schemed for his humiliation? He would never forgive me, you know that!"

"True," Alvaro nodded agreement, "but does it matter? Once you leave here you need never see him again."

She flinched, then swiftly lowered her lashes to hide the glint of tears. "Yes," she managed to whisper. "It matters, it matters terribly . . ."

Comprehension flashed across Alvaro's face as he expelled on a whispered breath, *"Madre de Dios!* You have not been foolish enough to fall in love with him?"

"It seems this is your night for bidding your ad-

169

mirers a last farewell!" Felipe's icy tone snaked out from the doorway. Sara's head jerked up, her tortured eyes flashing a mute yearning plea to be trusted, but when her look was met with glowering suspicion she turned and ran swiftly from the room, the sob catching in her throat sounding to Alvaro like the cry of a mortally wounded animal.

CHAPTER IX

ISABEL was chattering excitedly on and on, as she had done constantly since the announcement of the engagement and the swiftly advancing date of the wedding. They were in the small salon sorting through piles of patterns and batches of materials left there by the dressmaker who had been summoned to the villa by Doña Maria immediately she had been informed of their plans.

"Do you like this shade, Sara?" Isabel held a swathe of delicate blue organza against her sun-kissed complexion and waited for comment.

Sara tried to instil enthusiasm into her answer. "It is very becoming. Blue is a colour you should wear often."

Isabel gave a pleased nod and blushingly volunteered, "Alvaro said so, too, on the day he asked me to marry him. We were in the garden of my home in Catalonia," she confessed dreamily. "I had sensed weeks before that he intended to propose, so that day I purposely set out to make myself as attractive as possible in the hope that I might overcome his diffidence, and I succeeded beyond my wildest hopes."

"Shame on you for admitting to such guile!" Doña

Maria tried to look stern, but her lips twitched even as she reprimanded, "If I had known you were deliberately planning to ensnare my son I would never have agreed to Felipe sending him to work in your father's vineyards. Our intention was that he should go there to gain experience of the modern machinery recently installed there — not to be bombarded by wiles as old as Eve herself."

"Do you deny that you, too, were overjoyed when Alvaro told you of our betrothal?" Isabel met Doña Maria's twinkling eyes with serene complacency. "Indeed you cannot, because it was whispered to me by my mother that you had expressed just such a wish many years ago when Alvaro and I were mere babies."

Doña Maria was not in the least disconcerted. "Perhaps," she shrugged smilingly. "In the old days it was customary for families to choose their children's future partners when they were still mere infants. Nowadays, such action would not be tolerated by your modern generation, but it does not follow that we parents do not still hope and even, if the situation warrants, give a necessary push in the right direction."

All during the teasing interchange Sara listened with mounting dismay. Could it possibly be that Alvaro had lied when he accused Felipe and his mother of arranging a marriage for him behind his back? Isabel's words indicated that she had found no lack of ardour in a courtship Alvaro had denied ever existed! The thought of the wrong she might have done Felipe made her squirm inwardly; it was an effort to clear her throat and force out the question.

"I had no idea your courtship was of such long duration. How long have you been engaged, Isabel?"

"Simply *ages!*" she stressed, ignoring Doña Maria's tut-tut of denial. "You have no idea how fortunate you are to be marrying Felipe, who is a law unto himself, and who can make his own arrangements without fear of finding disfavour with his family. Alvaro and I were madly keen to be married six months ago, when he first proposed, but my family insisted upon us waiting so as to give them time to make arrangements for an elaborate affair which neither of us want. No wonder the poor dear took off in a temper and omitted even to write to me while he was away. Luckily," she smiled her relief, "Felipe was able to make him understand that the delay was a minor setback, a penance that had to be endured for the sake of keeping peace within the family, and so eventually he was persuaded to return." Suddenly she became pensive, the sparkle in her eyes dimmed by reflective memory. "I am grateful to Felipe," she stated soberly. "If it had not been for him I'm sure Alvaro would neither have forgiven nor understood."

When Doña Maria nodded agreement Sara realized with sudden insight the true extent of the debt they both owed to Felipe. Alvaro was their idol, in their eyes he could do no wrong, and because of that Felipe had never allowed them to discover the weaknesses that were only too apparent to those who knew his real character. She felt sickened by the lies that had tripped so lightly from his tongue, and by the way he had not hesitated to lay the blame for his own folly not only upon his cousin – whose back was broad – but also upon his mother. She wanted to berate them both for their stupidity, to tell them in no uncertain terms that the man they so readily excused had tried desperately to run away from his responsibilities towards the girl to whom he had proposed probably in a fit of pique or, what was even more likely, in an effort to relieve acute boredom. But of course she had to remain silent; the injustice she had so unknowingly done Felipe could not be rectified by destroying the peace of mind he had striven so hard to maintain. In a way, she could be grateful to Alvaro; if it were not for his lies she would not at this very moment be preparing for the wedding which was the outcome of Felipe's determination never to allow her to constitute a threat to the happiness of his family.

The following days passed in a nightmare rush of fittings with the dressmaker, whirlwind shopping bouts and the making of countless decisions ranging from the choosing of flowers for the bridal bouquet to the more mundane task of agreeing which sweet course should be served at the reception planned for the hundred or so guests who were to attend the wedding. Doña Maria had made herself responsible for drawing up the guest list which, at Sara's request, was cut to the very minimum. Even so, she was appalled by the number of

174

people Doña Maria solemnly insisted were so closely related that their presence was essential if family honour were to be upheld.

"But no one could possibly have so many close relatives!" she protested to the adamant Doña Maria.

The old lady's lips pursed obstinately. "Nonsense, child! This list is a mere fifth of the size it would be were Felipe not in such a hurry to claim his bride." She raised distrait eyebrows and wailed, "Two more weeks would have given me sufficient time to arrange things to perfection, but no, seven days were all I was allowed and, knowing Felipe, if matters are not concluded in the time stated he will disconcert us all by dispensing with ceremony completely!" This possibility seemed to spur her on to greater effort; she held out her hand for the list Sara was scanning with unbelieving eyes and stood with pencil poised as she urged, "I must have the names of the people you wish to invite. The caterer insists that he must have the final number by this evening at the latest."

Not for the first time in her life Sara regretted her orphaned state. She longed to be able to match Felipe's list with a formidable one of her own full of names guaranteed to assure his relatives of the solidarity of her background – but the wish was pointless yearning. "Marc Rochefort and Madame Blais are the only two I shall be inviting," she answered firmly, steeling herself for the surprised outburst she knew she could expect. It was quite a few seconds before Doña Maria found her voice, only to be cheated out of expressing her dismay by a firm request projected from the direction of the doorway.

"Can you spare Sara for a few minutes, Tia? There is something I wish to discuss with her." Coolly, Felipe swept her from under his aunt's nose and guided her outside to the deserted patio. She went unwillingly. For the past few days she had been attempting a meeting with Marc, only to be baulked at every turn by urgent demands upon her time from one or other of the family. These requests had been so well timed, and so seemingly spontaneous; she had been forced to accede to them and it had taken her until yesterday to realize that she was the victim of a conspiracy aimed at keeping Marc and herself apart. She had no doubt that its instigator was Felipe, and consequently her tone was cool when she rejected his offer of a seat.

"No, thank you, I prefer to stand," she tossed over her shoulder as she walked towards the edge of the pool, hoping the contemplation of its cool blue waters might calm her throbbing nerves.

"Come here, Sara," he insisted gently, making no move to approach her physically. She obeyed reluctantly. "That's better!" He smiled slightly as he led her towards a dual swing seat with a gay protective canopy and waited until she was seated before taking his place beside her. She showed little interest when he reached into his pocket to withdraw a small suede-covered box. With one lean finger he snapped open the catch and in spite of herself her eyes were drawn to examine the ring displayed upon a cushion of bridal white satin. It had an Arabian Nights quality, a possession worthy of a sultan or a king, a liquid emerald orb from which a thousand scintillating sparks ricocheted from a centre of molten green fire. Not for the life of her could she imagine herself walking around with such a king's ransom anchored to one small finger!

Her mute response seemed to please him. As he lifted up her hand to slip the priceless gem upon her finger he laughed softly and murmured, "So you feel it too – an aura of mystery, a feeling that if this ring could speak it might tell many tales of intrigue, of battles for possession fought and won so that the victor might carry to his lady love a jewel fine enough to express his devotion. See," he tilted her hand so that the sun's rays were caught and devoured by green flame, "once more it lives! Such jewels are fashioned by man for woman and only a woman's touch can bring forth their true beauty."

Her hand lay within his, limp and icily cold. A thrill of superstitious fear chilled her as she fought a conviction that the ancient ring, though harmless to lovers, might bring down the wrath of the gods upon any misuser. Their engagement made a mockery of love, the ring was to be a symbol of that mockery – what dire curse might it evoke as a revenge against their hypocrisy?

He frowned when he felt the shudder that ran

through her body. "What is it? Don't you like the ring?" She nodded, too miserably afraid to lie, then forced through tight lips.

"You are quite determined to go through with the wedding, aren't you, Felipe? What pleasure do you expect to derive from a marriage to someone you can never love?" He brooded down at her, deliberating her question but seeming in no hurry to put her out of her misery. A sudden flare of anger gave courage to her tongue, and an accusation was voiced even before the impulse had properly registered. "I am your weakness, Felipe, the only weakness you have ever allowed, and how you despise yourself for it! You want me so much physically that you are willing to overlook my less satisfying qualities, but is that a good enough basis for marriage? I've changed my mind! For both our sakes, I am breaking off our engagement now, before it is too late!"

Her words were as match to tinder. Vibrant emotion leapt to life in eyes that seconds before had been pools of inscrutability. He hissed through a tightly compressed mouth: "It is already too late! You are mine, *you belong to me!*" She was pulled fiercely forward to meet lips that descended to plunder with kisses so harsh she tried to cry out. He punished her revolt unmercifully, extracting what satisfaction he could from lips that refused to respond and from a body fighting desperately not to succumb to a wave of passion so devastating that the sun whirled in the heavens and the ground heaved beneath her feet. The answer she had goaded from him was growled against her fiery cheek. "Every man is entitled to one reckless impulse in his lifetime, *chica*, and marriage to you will be mine!"

He released his hold and she backed away, too overwhelmed by her own feelings to protest and too afraid of his to ever again chance being on the receiving end of a passion so intense that it overcame every civilized impulse. However suspect his motives, he was determined to make her his wife – he believed he had some prior claim over her . . . and in a strange, fatalistic way she believed it too! Had there been some tangle of magic in the potions heaped upon them both during the pagan marriage ceremony? By the powers of the mystic East she had been ordained a Rif bride and it seemed that any attempt she made to deny her subjugation only served to set the gods laughing . . .

She jumped up and ran from him, too shaken to protest further, her thoughts chaotic beyond reason, and was relieved when, after an aeon of silence, she heard his retreating footsteps resound against the tiled floor. She sagged against a pillar, relieved beyond measure that hostilities had momentarily ceased, and allowed tears of weakness to trickle down her ashen cheeks.

She was still there an hour later when Alvaro sought her out. His glance quickened as he noted the signs of inward torment her hour of solitude had not been able to erase and his tone was rough with apology even as he accused, "I warned you, did I not, what dire consequences might result from any clash with Felipe? Why didn't you heed my warning, Sara?" he pleaded with concern. "No one has ever yet managed to best him, as I know to my cost, but you can't say you went into the fight ignorant of his ruthless methods."

She seemed to stare blankly through him, so that for a second he was unsure if his words had registered, but she forced a flush to his face when she rebuked quietly, "I recognized the strength of my enemy, but not the treachery of my friend. Alvaro, why did you lie to me? I opposed Felipe on your behalf as much as my own because I thought you were being tyrannized into marriage against your will. None of this need ever have happened if you had been honest with me."

Alvaro grumbled, "I never intended to propose to Isabel. For weeks I was stuck on her parents' farm, driven almost to distraction by lack of amusement. Naturally, we were thrown together a lot, but I never meant to propose, it just sort of happened. If Felipe had kept out of my affairs the engagement would by now have died a natural death, but it was *he* who insisted upon reviving it; he even went to the extent of chasing me halfway around the world to make sure I would be here when Isabel came to visit. The damned girl would have been fixed up with someone else long ago if he had not insisted upon interfering!"

Sara flinched for Isabel. Doubtless he would now marry her – the engagement had been made public and not even he would have the effrontery to back out now

– but Isabel deserved a better future than was augured with a man of such doubtful qualities. She found herself praying that the blinkers would stay on, that Isabel would never be deprived of the rose-coloured glasses that portrayed for her a giant where others saw a pygmy.

Her response disguised her distaste sufficiently well to bring relief flooding back to Alvaro's face. "I don't think you realize how fortunate you are in your choice of bride, Alvaro, but perhaps that is something time will remedy. It is too late now for recriminations. We are in the same boat, you and I, both betrothed to partners whom neither of us deserve."

He looked shocked, as if the idea of himself being in any way inferior was a notion too ridiculous to be entertained, then he shrugged lightly and admitted, "Of late, I have become very much attracted to Isabel, so much so that the idea of marriage is no longer repugnant."

"I'm glad." Sara's smile warmed his chastened spirit. "I hope you will both be very happy."

"But what of you, *amada*?" he questioned solemnly. "What wish shall I make for you?"

"Wish for an armistice, Alvaro," she sighed wearily. "All I can hope for now are reasonable terms of surrender . . ."

CHAPTER X

THE ancient, beautiful church seemed crowded to
capacity as Sara was escorted down the aisle on the
arm of Felipe's uncle. A thousand eyes were trained
upon her pale, very lovely face framed by a veil of
Spanish lace that had been worn throughout generations by every Panza bride. They assessed with approval her slight figure, looking in virginal white an insubstantial shadow as she glided past columns of black
marble and oak-panelled walls towards the man who
waited, gravely erect, until she reached his side. That
her brilliant eyes were stunned passed without comment; it was fitting that she should be so aware of the
extent of her good fortune. Felipe was, after all, the
most eligible bachelor in the whole of Morocco.

She moved in a dream through the sea of faces that
were turned so eagerly towards her, but clung to the
sight of cherubic choirboys whose sweet voices soared
high up to the domed ceiling in a hymn of praise that
fitted her fantasy perfectly. The moment had actually
arrived. For days now she had accepted that the inevitable must happen, she had ceased fighting against Felipe's domination and had allowed herself to float upon
a tide of events which in the last days had developed
into a flood. Now on the final wave, she was being cast

up like a piece of flotsam at the feet of the man she was preparing, once more, to marry. An hysterical giggle rose in her throat as she wondered lightheadedly what effect the news that this was to be the second marriage ceremony they had participated in would have upon Felipe's starchy relatives. But the giggle died into a quiet gasp as, with a final reassuring squeeze, Felipe's uncle relinquished his hold upon her hand before passing it over into his nephew's firm keeping.

She dared a look at him, but immediately swept her lashes down over cheeks that were suddenly hot. She barely followed the ceremony; her confused mind was grappling with the magnitude of feeling she had glimpsed in that one quick look, and her senses whirled as she fearfully acknowledged that the odd flashes of feeling he occasionally allowed to escape him were the mere tip of an iceberg that, should it ever melt, would create devastation.

He put on a very convincing act for the benefit of his family. His responses were spoken firmly, but with an undertone of reverence that amazed her – in direct contrasted to her own which stumbled out in inaudible gasps – and his compelling eyes were upon her face during the whole of the service. During the reception he was understandably attentive. As they stood together to receive the congratulations and good wishes of their guests his arm encircled her waist and every now and then when a fit of trembling seized her his grasp tightened to communicate understanding and reassurance while at the same time his eyes forced her into sharing glances so intimate that she felt unbelievably cherished. His attitude was unbearably tantalizing. She yearned to be able to relax, to bask in his unaccustomed approval, but the certainty that once the guests had gone and they were again alone together he would revert to treating her as an expensive toy made her determined to remain aloof.

When he was called away to take a telephone message the relief from pressure was tremendous. So much so that when Marc seized the opportunity to speak to her he was dazzled by the welcome he received.

"Marc!" she almost stammered in her eagerness. "I'm so glad you managed to come."

"Did you ever doubt that I would?" he smiled, his eyebrows elevating with teasing enquiry. Then his smile was replaced by grave sincerity. "You look enchanting, Sara, ravishingly beautiful. I should hate Felipe for stealing you away from me, but I must admit in all honesty that you were never really mine." He sighed, then shook himself free of abortive regrets. "We had lunch together yesterday, Felipe and I, did you know?" Surprise robbed her of speech, so he nodded and continued, "Yes, we spent a most rewarding hour in each other's company. I no longer have any doubts about your choice of husband, *chérie*. If I cannot have you then there is no other I would rather see in my place. Be happy, Sara," he whispered quickly as he saw Felipe's advancing figure, "and think of me sometimes . . ."

He melted into the crowd before she could question his amazing change of opinion, and all during the ensuing rush to change into travelling clothes and even while she and Felipe ran the gauntlet of happy guests determined to give a hearty send-off to the honeymoon she was frantically wondering what confidences exchanged between the two men had resulted in dissolving their initial animosity to the extent of leaving them firm friends.

The villa where they were to begin their honeymoon was perched high upon a cliff overlooking a tiny bay. On either side of the bay promontories of rock ensured complete privacy; the beach being accessible only from steps cut out of the sheer cliff face. It belonged to a member of Felipe's family who had put it at their disposal for an indefinite period, insisting that they would be favouring him by making use of its amenities and by providing work for the two Arab boys he employed as servants. Darkness had fallen by the time they arrived, after a silent journey along a coast road which every now and then had offered glimpses of black velvet sea heaving under a scattering of glistening silver moonbeams. Her nervousness was very obvious, and Felipe's straight-cut mouth quirked upwards when, as he pulled up in front of the villa, her startled eyes leapt to his face, then hastily away again.

"Shall I carry you across the threshold, or would you prefer to walk?" he enquired dryly when she made no move to abandon the car. Hastily she scrambled from her seat, almost tripping in her eagerness to escape the underlying threat. Her face burned as his soft laughter reached her through the darkness and she bit her lip to prevent frightened tears from falling. She was too overwrought to admire the quiet opulence of the interior of the villa, and he frowned when she spun round in startled confusion when the Arab servant, whose approach had been silent, enquired whether they were ready to eat. In response to the questioning lift of Felipe's eyebrows she shook her head, then had grave misgivings when she heard him tell the boy that his services would not be required until morning.

She was standing by the window, tense as a bowstring, when he approached from behind to urge her kindly, "You are tired and not a little tense. Why don't you go to your room – a bath will relax you and later, when I've had my swim, I'll bring you up a drink that will help you to sleep."

Fear loosened her tongue. "Swim? In the dark . . .?"

Laughter was a low rumble in his throat. "But yes, do you find that so unusual? I often swim by moonlight."

Her wariness of water dated far back to the days in the orphanage when swimming had been allowed only under strict supervision and certainly in the broad light of day when any unforeseen danger could be spotted and swiftly averted.

"But there might be currents – and the cliff looks so terribly steep . . ." She faltered to a stop, her eyes

186

enormous. Suddenly he was very close, too close for peace of mind. Her body was suffused by fire when against her ear she felt the feathering of his lips as he breathed,

"And if I should break my neck tumbling down the cliff, or suffer any other of the unmentionable fears that are spinning through your mind, would you care, *cara* . . . ?"

She spun away from him, too agitated to think clearly, and so humiliated by his amusement her only defence was to lash back with words. "Go for your swim!" she choked as she retreated in confusion. "I could not care less whatever the outcome may be!" But once in her room restless pacing gave lie to her hasty words. She was tormented by fears for his safety, but too proud and too sensitive of his laughter to do as her senses urged and fly out into the night in search of him. She forced herself to undress and take a shower, then with a negligée wrapped loosely around her, she sat staring into a mirror as she brushed her hair, seeing nothing of her fear-whitened face, but concentrating on every little sound coming from outside that might tell her he had returned safely. She heard the Arab boys talking quietly together as they set off towards the nearby village where their families lived, but for a long time afterwards no sound disturbed the still night and as the silence grew her fears were magnified out of all proportion. She glanced down at the great emerald she was agitatedly twisting around her finger and shivered; the green, cold stare could have come from the malevolent eye of Yiblis himself as he debated her punishment. She began to picture Felipe's lithe body lying crushed and broken at the foot of the hungry cliff, and a sob broke from her as she recalled hearing tales of strong swimmers being crippled by cramp, of others whose bodies had been tossed on distant shores after fighting a losing battle with vicious currents.

Rif superstition held her so fast in its grip that she failed to hear a light tap upon her door. When she did not reply Felipe entered quietly, carrying a tray holding a decanter and two glasses. He was wearing a silk dressing-gown, his hair roughly towelled but still glistening with sea-water. He glanced immediately over the curves of her body outlined by transparent white chiffon, but when his eyes lifted to her set features he frowned darkly. Quickly, he disposed of the tray and strode tight-lipped across the width of the room to take her by the shoulders. "*Madre de Dios!*" he hissed. "You have no need to look like that. I swear I have no intention of harming you!"

His demented words shocked her back to life and when she lifted tortured eyes to his face and whispered brokenly: "Oh, Felipe, thank God you are safe!" she betrayed a secret so momentous that a few taut, amazed seconds were necessary before complete understanding dawned. Then: "Sara ... you really were afraid for me! Oh, my beloved, my own dearest love!" He moved with the speed of light, wasting no more words, but gathering her up into an embrace that speared shivers of delight through her pliant body. Kisses of mingled longing and remorse were stormed upon her quivering mouth, her tear-wet cheeks, and tender, painfully aching throat. When she was allowed to, she whispered, "Felipe, I don't understand, you can't love me, it isn't possible ..." Protests that were silenced with typical Spanish arrogance without deigning even to afford them the importance of a denial. Then gradually, his kisses grew less wild and full of tender sweetness and she began to believe that the pinnacle of hope she had never dared aspire to was not merely a possibility but glorious reality. He caressed her with restrained ardour, whispering broken phrases of love that reached her through the growing heat of ecstasy, treating her with the gentle reverence of a passion deliberately leashed, by great power of will, so that fear should play no part in the final, glorious consummation both physical and spiritual. He understood completely her shy uncertainty; his demands were kind, his insistence tender, and he was rewarded by the breaking down of every last doubt as she surrendered entirely to the love he had demonstrated was as great and as unselfish as her own. The pounding of the sea became a roar that filled the room as she was lifted against his heart and carried towards fulfilment – the destiny ordained by the gods of the Rif who must at that very moment have been smiling ...

She was supremely happy, contentedly relaxed as she

toyed idly with the medallion nestling amongst the tangle of dark hairs that grew across his chest. "How long have you loved me, Felipe?" she questioned with pretended casualness. She heard him growl a laugh, then thrilled to his nearness as his bulk towered over her in the darkness.

"How like a woman!" he mocked. "Not satisfied with having ensnared me completely, you want the time, date and moment of my downfall. Does it matter, *cara*?" he nuzzled her throat. "Isn't the fact that our love exists sufficiently wonderful to fill your heart and mind for many years to come?"

She dimpled in the darkness. "Of course, but women like to be practical . . ."

"Curious, you mean," he contradicted with mock disgust.

But with all the rashness of Eve, she pressed him, confident he would deny her nothing. "Tell me . . ." she pleaded. He went very still. She immediately sensed his withdrawal and was appalled by her lack of sensitivity when she recognized the extent of the hurt she had so wilfully resurrected.

"I have always loved you," he told her with difficulty. "From the very first moment we met I was attracted, but I would not admit it even to myself." His arms reached out as if even now he was afraid she might try to escape, when he admitted, "You know how I misjudged you, my sweet Sara. I was a fool, a cretinous idiot, but even while I fought the emotion you aroused in me I was certain, deep down in my heart, that you were the only woman I could ever love." Her small surprised gasp caused him to tighten his hold, her closeness giving him comfort, as he relived a moment of agony. "It took a horde of galloping horses to drive home just how much you really meant to me," he murmured huskily. "If you had died beneath their hooves that day, my darling, my life would have ended in that same second. From that moment on I tried to heal the breach between us, but our every meeting was at sword's point and no matter how much I tried each attempted victory ended in defeat. I knew you hated me because of my treatment of your grandfather, and because of the drastic measures I had to employ to prevent you from slipping out of my grasp. Finally, I had to resort to intimidation in my bid to keep you near me." She smiled secretly at the hint of puzzlement in his voice when he pondered aloud, "My greatest surprise was when you agreed to my proposal. Overjoyed as I was, I could not understand why you did not immediately throw my offer of marriage back in my face! "

"But you are no longer puzzled, are you, my darling?" she teased, preparing herself for the retaliation she knew would follow. He did not disappoint her, and for a time conversation ceased while he chastised her with kisses. Wrapped in the warmth of his love, she could think of her grandfather without pain, and perhaps he sensed this when he chose that moment to speak of him again.

"I have Marc to thank for releasing me from my self-imposed purgatory. He explained many things that had puzzled me – he also told me about the circumstances surrounding your life with your grandfather." He paused, fighting a return of the hard anger he had felt when Marc had outlined the Colonel's shameless exploitation of his granddaughter's affection. She was not deceived by his silence; some day she might endeavour to make him understand, but at that moment all she could manage were the choked words: "He was a good man, Felipe, and I loved him dearly ..." She waited, willing his anger to die, fearful that even now some spectre from the past might spoil the wonder of their love. Impulsively, she reached out to draw his head down against her breast and for long minutes he fought a silent battle she was not allowed to share. Finally, his mind at war, he startled her by grating out one last tormented question.

"Did you ever really want to marry Alvaro?"

"You need to ask me that ... now?" she trembled, her obvious distress dissolving for ever the last shadow of misunderstanding that had plagued them. A great sigh rippled through his taut frame before he swept her close and muttered through mounting passion, "We have talked long enough, *cara!*" Eagerly, she opened her arms to receive him, and as she lifted her slender hand to caress his dark head with a possessiveness he adored the emerald upon her finger glittered, then flared suddenly into glorious, dazzling life.